PRAISE FOR

Come Together, Fall Apart

"Luminous . . . Each story is full of subtle surprises and unexpected twists." —*San Francisco Chronicle*

"Henríquez creates a vision of Panama that is at once sweepingly realistic and subtly hallucinogenic. Losses great and small are common currency, and yet these fluid stories abound in beauty, irony, and magic. Like Junot Diaz and Daniel Alarcón, Henríquez is an immensely gifted young writer who evokes the spirit of a struggling land and the people who love it beyond reason."

—*Booklist* (starred review)

"[A] dazzling new talent. Henríquez's voice is artfully simple and unembellished, soft yet quietly piercing. . . . Compassionate, tender, and fresh." —*Kirkus Reviews* (starred review)

"Henríquez shows great promise. . . . [She] finds the pulse of Panama without having been born there. After reading *Come Together, Fall Apart*, you'd swear she had lived there her entire life." —*Fort Worth Star-Telegram*

"How does a young writer gather the wisdom, heart, and tenderness to write stories of such exquisite humanity? I can only guess she is an ancient soul, a Zen master, a *bruja*, or all of the above. However it's done, I bow deeply and welcome this first collection." —Sandra Cisneros, author of
The House on Mango Street and *Caramelo*

continued . . .

Come Together, Fall Apart

a novella and stories

CRISTINA HENRÍQUEZ

Riverhead Books
New York

THE BERKLEY PUBLISHING GROUP
Published by the Penguin Group
Penguin Group (USA) Inc.
375 Hudson Street, New York, New York 10014, USA
Penguin Group (Canada), 90 Eglinton Avenue East, Suite 700, Toronto, Ontario M4P 2Y3, Canada (a division of
Pearson Penguin Canada Inc.)
Penguin Books Ltd, 80 Strand, London WC2R 0RL, England
Penguin Group Ireland, 25 St Stephen's Green, Dublin 2, Ireland (a division of Penguin Books Ltd)
Penguin Group (Australia), 250 Camberwell Road, Camberwell, Victoria 3124, Australia (a division of Pearson
Australia Group Pty. Ltd.)
Penguin Books India Pvt. Ltd., 11 Community Centre, Panchsheel Park, New Delhi—110 017, India
Penguin Group (NZ), Cnr Airborne and Rosedale Roads, Albany, Auckland 1310, New Zealand (a division of
Pearson New Zealand Ltd)
Penguin Books (South Africa) (Pty) Ltd, 24 Sturdee Avenue, Rosebank, Johannesburg 2196, South Africa

Penguin Books Ltd., Registered Offices: 80 Strand, London WC2R 0RL, England

This is a work of fiction. Names, characters, places, and incidents either are the product of the author's imagina-
tion or are used fictitiously, and any resemblance to actual persons, living or dead, business establishments,
events, or locales is entirely coincidental. The publisher does not have any control over and does not assume any
responsibility for author or third-party websites or their content.

Acknowledgment is made to the publications in which these stories first appeared: "Drive" in *The Virginia Quarterly Review;* "Ashes" in *The New Yorker;* "Mercury" in *Glimmer Train;* "Beautiful" in *TriQuarterly.*

First Riverhead hardcover edition: April 2006
First Riverhead trade paperback edition: April 2007
Riverhead trade paperback ISBN: 978-1-59448-241-0

The Library of Congress has catalogued the Riverhead hardcover edition as follows:

Henríquez, Cristina, date.
Come together, fall apart : a novella and stories / by Cristina Henríquez.
p. cm.
ISBN 1-59448-915-7
1. Panama—Social life and customs—Fiction. 2. Young women—Fiction. I. Title.
PS3608.E5675C66   2006   2005050848
813'.6—dc22

Printed in the United States of America
10 9 8 7 6 5 4 3 2 1

FOR MY FAMILY

Contents

Come Together, Fall Apart

Yanina

Yanina has asked me to marry her forty-five times. Sometimes she makes elaborate plans before she proposes. Like last time: She gathered broken crab legs and laid them on the sand to spell MARRY ME, RENÉ, in English and everything. At least that's what she told me. By the time she convinced me to go to the beach, the tide had come in enough to wash away half of it so all that was left was MAR RENÉ, and I was like, Yeah, I *know* it's the ocean, you didn't have to drag me all the way down here to tell me that. She started crying right there. She's very emotional like that. She tried to explain through tears and little bubbles of saliva that she wanted to marry me. More than anything in the world, that's what she wanted. I know, *mami*, I told her and held her close, her sea-salt hair rough against my face. Then why don't you? she moaned into my chest. Soon, I said, which is what I always say. She looked at me with puffy, red eyes. I thought she was going to start crying again. But instead, she got mean. You should shave off that mustache, she said. It makes you look so stupid. I knew she was only trying to hurt me because I had hurt her. Her brand of meanness was of the temperate variety. She threw little punches but they were never the sort to leave bruises. Come on, I said, and bent down. She stuck out her lip but then climbed on, hooked her legs around my waist, her arms around my neck, and I carried her off the beach, up the dirt road to our house.

We got this house in El Rompío from Yanina's godfather, Mauricio de Bernal. He left for the United States last year and told Yanina she could use it when she wanted. When she lost her job at a department store called Mattito's a few weeks ago, we decided to split Panama City and land here for a while. I was at university, out of school for the summer break, anyway. It's nice—far from the city. There's one restaurant, a convenience shop, and a few older couples who rent or own the handful of houses that exist out here. We met a neighbor named Diego when we first arrived. He lives with his aunt, but we haven't seen him—or any other neighbors—since. Who knows how long we'll stay, but I don't ask questions because either Yanina will go, You want to stay longer? and that will get her hopes up, or else she'll say, You want to leave already? and that will make her mad.

The worst thing about this setup is that Yanina makes us sleep in separate rooms. She insists. On our drive out, she went on and on about respect for her godfather, who is a churchgoing man, the real deal, Jesus' blood in his veins and everything. If we slept in the same bed before we were married, apparently, according to him, it would be a sin. Even so, the first night we were here I tried to climb into bed next to her. I thought it was worth a shot. The sheets were thin and musty and I had to step over a hoard of ants huddled on a sweet spot on the floor just to get to her. I lay down and put my arm over her waist, fitting my knees into the bend of hers, feeling our skin stick together lightly. A few minutes later Yanina shifted and said, Okay, back to your room now. There was no talking her out of it. She kept lecturing me about loyalty to her *padrino*, saying he wouldn't have wanted it in his house. She loved him a lot, that man. He was like a father to her in certain ways. When she was growing up, her own father had run off with a

Dominican woman and then died a few years later. What could I do? I went to another bedroom, one where the bed sagged so much along one side that I had to push it into a corner and sleep touching the concrete wall to avoid rolling off during the night. The wall was cool against my skin, but I would rather have been pressed against the shimmering warmth of Yanina.

Now I get up early in the morning, when a sweep of ocean mist still hangs in the air, and go to her room to watch her sleeping. Usually she's completely under the covers—head and everything—and by now, I know just where to peel back the sheet to reveal her face. She has a tiny body, though it's not without its meat. Mostly in her hips, and she has a little bit of a belly. Her breasts are small. I can cover the whole of one with my hand. She lets me do that once in a while when we're lying side by side; she'll take my hand and guide it up to her chest—a chest like a little bird's—letting me cup my palm over her breast, her pale nipple. It feels so good to touch her like that.

Sometimes I don't know why I haven't asked her yet. What's stopping me. It's like there's an invisible wall. I keep walking forward, thinking I can step right into a new future, but I run into that wall every time, without knowing that it's there, without being able to say what it looks like. Then other times I see everything crystal clear: I'm not ready yet, I'm not sure about her, I don't know if what we have is enough to stand up to a whole life. But I never say these things out loud.

She's awake now and making breakfast. I go to help but she's trying to prove something. She fries thick slices of ham and lays them on toast, then drenches the whole thing in honey.

"Good," I tell her, chewing.

She looks pleased.

"How's your book?" I ask. She's reading about graphic design. She's trying to carve out her path in this life, she's told me. Mattito's was just a stopover.

"I'm reading about type," she says.

"Does it mention me?"

"What?"

"You know, how I'm your type." I grin. I'm studying business at university. I can't get what she's doing. She always loved art. She used to sketch all the time in this little green notebook. She did me once. My face came out kind of lopsided and flat-looking but she said that was the style. At some point I guess she realized there was no money in art, and graphic design was booming in Panama. So she got on the computer.

Yanina puts her hands on her hips. "You don't have to be such a clown *all the time*, René."

I push the chewed bread up between my lips and teeth and smile at her, the honeyed mush peeking out like doughy gums.

She can't help herself. She cracks up, her face ablaze with laughter until the top mash of bread falls out and plops onto the table.

"You're cleaning that up," she says, but she's still smiling.

After breakfast, I go check on the dogs. They came with the house. We saw them when we first pulled up—two skinny brown hounds tied to concrete poles and barking at us. We assumed they'd been left behind, whether by accident or on purpose it was hard to tell. But we tossed food between the poles to calm them. Yanina started by throwing pieces of bread straight from the plastic sleeve. They're not ducks, I told her. So we flung chicken on the ground and they ate it, bones and all. I named them: Perro and Perron. I check on them every day. Yanina thinks it's good for me, like having kids. I let them loose one at a time so they can get some exercise.

"Which one's the girl?" Yanina asks today, through the window, as I'm unleashing Perro.

I point to Perron. The leash buckle is rusted and I have to pull hard to get it to come undone.

"You should let the girl go first!" Yanina shouts. She's doing dishes in the kitchen. I hear the water sloshing. "That would be polite."

"I don't think dogs are really into chivalry, you know?" I yank again on the leash and it falls off Perro's neck. He's probably a hundred yards away already by the time I look back over my shoulder, through the screen window, to see Yanina frowning at me.

"Come on," I say. "They don't know the difference."

"What's the girl's name?"

"Perron."

"Evita," Yanina says, smiling.

I'm not sure I heard her or maybe she didn't hear me. "Her name's Perron," I say again.

"Right. <u>Eva Perón</u>." Yanina laughs. She thinks this is a funny joke. "That's what I'm going to call her from now on—Eva."

My girl's so stupid, I think. It's the dumbest thing I've ever heard. But it makes me smile, too. "Eva Perón died of cancer, you know."

"René," Yanina says, "you're so sweet sometimes. You know that? You should hear me telling my mamá about you. Mami, he's such a nice boy! And he always knows just the right thing to say." She smiles sarcastically and leans across the sink, pressing her face against the inside of the screen, making her caramel skin into tiny grids where it touches. "Don't you want to get married, *mi amor*?" She presses her lips flat like flower petals. They're some gorgeous shell-colored lips.

I could say yes. I could say it right now, I think. I

could walk out of one life and into the next just like that.

"Soon," I tell her at last. Eva Perón barks sharply.

"Eva thinks it's a good idea," Yanina says.

"Eva said 'soon,' too."

"You speak dog now?" Yanina gazes at me for a few seconds, her dark eyelashes so long they nearly brush against the metal screen. Then she walks away, out of the frame of the window. Just leaves. Maybe she goes to her bedroom to get under the sheet and contemplate everything like she does when she's sad. Or maybe to the car, where she escapes to cry because she doesn't want me to hear her.

Eva nudges her head against my arm.

"What?" I ask.

She lifts her paws and lowers them again, prancing in place, and just stares at me with her glassy eyes.

Yanina and I met at Restaurante Boulevard. I went in for a strawberry milk shake and this friend of mine, Graciela, saw me and told me to come sit. That was the first time I saw Yanina. She was small behind the table, her hair coiled in a plastic clip. She didn't make too much of an impression. Graciela and I talked about whatever; I don't even remember now. But I recall perfectly this moment when Graciela started laughing because some of my milk shake had collected on my upper lip and was in my mustache.

"Why do you have that thing, anyway?" Graciela asked. "No one has mustaches anymore."

Yanina giggled. "It's to make up for the hair that's missing from his scraggly eyebrows."

I shot her a look. She'd hardly said anything up to that point and she didn't even know me. Graciela practically fell on the floor laughing. Yanina didn't look pleased with herself, though. She looked sorry. I knew then that she was complicated. That didn't help her cause. I didn't usually go for the complicated ones. And she'd insulted me, too. So when Graciela mentioned a party and asked if I could drive Yanina there, I said no. Graciela kicked me under the table. I guessed she was trying to set us up. I didn't want it to be like that, though. I looked at Yanina and said, "You need a chauffeur? At your service." Graciela kicked me again.

When I picked Yanina up, she was wearing a low-cut sparkling purple dress. Under the streetlamps, the light danced off her like a disco ball.

"I didn't know it was that kind of party," I said when she got in the car. I was wearing blue jeans and a T-shirt.

"Maybe I'm just that kind of girl," she said.

"What kind?" I pulled the car away from the curb.

"The—" she started. She looked out the window. "The kind who wants to look nice for a party?"

"Okay," I said.

We were quiet after that. She kept making little noises like she wanted to say something, but then she wouldn't. I didn't have much interest in starting a conversation anyway.

We were near a small bridge about ten minutes from the party when Yanina said, "My father died on a bridge." She said it to the window.

I thought she meant he jumped off, but I don't know why. "Really?" I said.

"He was a construction worker. A car hit him."

I had no idea why she was telling me this.

"It didn't knock him off, though. He just died there on the pavement." She still had her face turned from me.

I squeezed my hands around the steering wheel. "I'm sorry."

She didn't say anything back. I wondered what her face looked like then. I wished she would turn to me but she didn't. I hoped to Christ she wasn't crying.

"Mamá and I heard about it from his other woman. She called us. We didn't even know he had another woman until then. Some Dominican I guess he was seeing."

I felt like there was something I was supposed to say,

some perfect thing that a person better than me would be able to come up with.

"I'm sorry," I said again.

She shrugged.

At the <u>party, later that night</u>, she asked me to marry her for the <u>first time</u>.

In the afternoon, we go to the market—really just a four-aisle store with fruit and vegetables in wooden crates along the walls, canned food, warm soda, bread, bags of pork rinds, huge sacks of rice piled near the door, and a small freezer with frosty packages of meat and tubs of concrete butter. The old woman who works there is constantly knitting a scarf for her son in the United States. "He's in New York," she tells us proudly almost every time we go.

"In New York," she says today, "there is an enormous park, as big as Brazil, right in the middle of the city."

"Brazil is pretty big," I tell her as I rummage through the freezer for a package of ground beef.

I find one that looks good and take it to the register. When I put it down, its icy underbelly makes it skate slowly across the countertop. Yanina has an assortment of cans and bags—food for the week. She still hasn't said a word to me since walking away from the window earlier. When I told her I was coming here, all she did was march out of the house and get in the car, keeping her arms crossed the whole way over. Everything crackles and thuds as she drops it on the counter.

"And the women!" The old woman smiles, shaking her head. "Like they should be in beauty pageants, my son says. All young and blond!"

"I like the women here," I say, looking at Yanina. Then I turn to the old woman. "They're the most beautiful no matter what their age."

The woman blushes and grins. I feel good, being able to make her smile. Yanina raises her eyebrows at me and walks out, leaving me to carry the bags on my own.

When we arrive back at the house, a small brown car is parked in front.

"Are you expecting company?" I ask.

She shakes her head but part of me wonders whether the car is a new plan Yanina has concocted, like it belongs to a guy delivering balloons that I'll have to pop and inside one will be a ring. I half expect to see someone jump out of a cake when we walk in the house but instead I am greeted by a girl about my age and a man, both seated at the kitchen table, where they are playing cards. A wire cage holding flitting yellow birds sits on the floor.

"They are parakeets," the man says, pointing to the birds when he sees me eyeing them. He's older, with full, charcoal-colored hair brushed straight back over his head. His eyelids droop and he wears rumpled clothes that look like they're left over from the seventies.

"What?" I say. I'm cradling the brown bags from the market in my arms. I want to ask what the hell he's doing in our house.

"They are parakeets," he says again.

I peer over my shoulder at Yanina, who, I realize, stopped walking a few steps behind me and hasn't moved since. I give her a questioning glance.

She stares past me to the man in our kitchen and slowly a smile spreads over her face.

"Tío Mauricio," she says.

The man, who I now gather is Mauricio de Bernal, smiles back, his heavy eyes sinking into his face. I expect one of them to make a move to hug the other but Yanina just stands there grinning stupidly and Mauricio de Bernal sits there grinning back and I am standing there holding the groceries and the girl at the table is straightening the cards in her hands shyly, not looking at anyone, and the birds are chirping lightly, oblivious to it all.

Finally I stride over and, under the weight of the bags, extend my hand. "It's nice to meet you, after all this time," I say. I'm on my best behavior, for Yanina.

He shakes my hand but he says, "And *who* are you, may I inquire?"

"René Calderón."

"René Calderón," he repeats thoughtfully. "It finds a pleasurable place on the tongue, though it is not a name I am familiar with."

I'm waiting for Yanina to tell him that I'm her guy, you know, her boyfriend, but instead she makes her way to the table and says, "I can't believe you're here. When did you get back?" She directs her questions to Mauricio de Bernal only, entirely ignoring the girl at the table.

I put the bags down. One of the dogs outside starts barking and then the other joins in. This makes the birds start flapping their tiny wings and they dart from one side of the cage to the other, tweeting and crisscrossing each other in the air.

Mauricio de Bernal asks for a dish towel. When I hand him one, he drapes it over the cage. The birds quiet, twittering softly to themselves in the dark.

"We've taken care of the dogs," Yanina says.

Mauricio de Bernal shakes his head. "I could not bring them with me," he says, as if it's something he thinks about—and regrets—every day. "I told your mother they were here. She was to care for them if you did not. But I expected you would."

The girl sets her stack of cards on the table and says, "Excuse me, I need to go to the bathroom." She has a peculiar accent.

Yanina looks at her, startled. I point the girl down the hall toward the bathroom. She is thin and tall, with fine brown hair the color of cardboard cut in layers that hang around her face. Her cheeks are pinkish and her skin very pale.

"That is Charlotte," Mauricio de Bernal offers. He has trouble pronouncing the name and stutters a few times before giving up and saying it in Spanish: Carlota.

Yanina whispers, "Are you together?"

Mauricio de Bernal laughs from a place deep in his stomach, squeezing his eyes shut. "She is my daughter," he says.

"What?"

"From the United States. I had a daughter. I was unaware, all these years, that she existed. But it is the reason I went—to find her. Her mother told me of her. I had little hope she would want to see me, though. I prayed every day. But only God knows how things will turn out. So I did not tell anyone before I left. In case I had to come back and report bad news."

"I don't understand," Yanina says.

Mauricio de Bernal takes her hand in his, kneading it with his thumbs. "I have a daughter," he says again as if now, the second time, this explains everything.

Yanina stares at him for a few sustained seconds before she starts blinking fast, a sure sign that she's about to cry.

Charlotte walks back into the kitchen and hesitates before taking a seat at the table. Yanina stares at her.

Charlotte says "Hey," softly.

Yanina is blinking like crazy now and the tip of her nose is blooming red. She stands, yanking her hand from Mauricio de Bernal, and walks to where I've laid the bags. She starts pulling out the cans and the snacks and the meat wrapped in Styrofoam and shoves it all into cabinets and into the rusty green refrigerator, everything scraping and bumping and slamming and making a whole big riot. I want to go to her, put my arms around her shoulders, stop her from moving for just one second. But if I went to her, I know, she would shrug me off. In the middle of her despair, she needs to be alone. She'll come to me later.

"*Hija,*" Mauricio de Bernal says plaintively, but she just hurries out, sprinting for her bedroom and closing the door behind her.

The second time she asked me was at the start of the new year. By then we were, as her mother liked to say, inchy-pinchy. Some guys she knew were doing fireworks in Panama la Vieja. Buildings that used to stand tall there, hundreds of years earlier, were little more than broken skeletons of themselves now. It reminded me of

El Chorillo, the area of the city destroyed by the Americans during the invasion, more than a decade ago.

We sat on a pile of huge, weathered stones. All over the city, little poppers were going off, kids shooting them into the night. People dotted the grass below us. High in the sky, the fireworks sprouted arms and fell, breaking apart in the air.

At one point there was a long pause and people started grumbling, thinking it was over without the usual grand finale. But then something whistled and exploded and a trail of light burned an *R* into the inky sky. A few seconds later, the finale started. Hundreds of fireworks all at once, crackling above us, leaving puffs of pastel smoke hanging in the air.

Yanina turned to me. "That was for you, René," she said.

I must have looked at her dumbly because she said, "The *R*. It was for your name. I couldn't pay for the rest of the letters."

"You paid them to do that?"

She nodded. "Ricardo got me a discount, though."

"Why?"

"He's a good friend. He didn't want me to pay full price."

"No. I mean, about me."

She looked like she was considering this but all she said was, "Maybe next year I'll get you an *E*."

"Good thing my name's not longer. This could take a lifetime."

"René," she said suddenly, turning to me, "will you marry me?"

I started laughing. I remembered when she had asked me the same thing, though with much less fanfare and much less seriousness, on the roof of her friend's apartment, where we had gone to a party together. Only then I assumed it was just because she was drunk.

"Maybe," I said.

"You'll ask me soon, won't you?"

"Soon," I said, just to say it.

She was crazy, I thought then. Absolutely nuts. Already, though, I had learned to love that about her.

The first night Mauricio de Bernal and Charlotte are there Yanina and I stand outside. I try to draw her out. What's wrong, *mami?* Tell me what's going on with you. She's been carrying on all day. She tells me what's already obvious. All this about how Mauricio is like her father, how she's always been taught to think of him that way, and how he never had children of his own so he had loved Yanina because she was like a daughter to him, only now he has a real daughter, flesh and blood, so what use does he have for Yanina anymore, and already things are changing between them, and on and on. I try to tell her that's ridiculous. It isn't like he can only love one person at a time. It isn't like there's a hole in his world in the shape of a daughter and once Charlotte steps into it, she automatically shoves Yanina out. And you shouldn't hold it against Charlotte, I say, because she seems like a nice enough girl who just met her father and is in a new country and she hasn't done anything to you. At that, Yanina hits me. Really wallops me on my arm.

"What?" I ask, rubbing the spot.

Yanina shakes her head like it is so exasperating to have to deal with me.

After a while, I have her calmed down but the drama starts again when Mauricio de Bernal tells Charlotte to sleep in Yanina's room. I hear Yanina trying to convince her *padrino* that there isn't enough room in the bed for the two of them.

"But it is a double bed," Mauricio de Bernal argues.

Yanina says, "She could sleep outside with Perro and Eva."

"The dogs?" Mauricio asks. "On the ground?"

"No?" Yanina says. Though I can't see her, I can imagine her blinking fast, her jaw tight. "Because she's special? You left the dogs behind and now you'll leave me behind, but she is special, you know." I know she has just flung her hand in the air. I recognize that tone. I am sure, too, that Charlotte is somewhere, hearing this as I am.

"Yanina, *hija*. She's—"

"She's your daughter. I know. *She* is."

Before she can get out anything else, I go, take her elbow, and drag her into the bathroom. She is a mess. "I hate her," Yanina says.

"Listen—"

"Why did he have to bring her here?"

"Charlotte sleeps in my bed—" I put my hand up before she can protest, "and I sleep in your bed. With you."

She doesn't even flinch. "Okay," she says.

One week later and there's no sign of Mauricio de Bernal or Charlotte leaving. It's close quarters. Yanina's been angling to spend time with Mauricio but he's kept busy taking Charlotte on long walks, showing her the spots of his youth and whatever.

Today, after seven days of the birds shrieking at all hours, Mauricio de Bernal decides to let them loose in the house. This requires closing all the windows and doors without screens to make sure the birds don't escape. He's worried because they haven't been eating any of their seed lately. But when he opens the cage, they don't budge. Some of them look at him wonderingly and cock their heads, and the rest ignore the escape route altogether.

I try to read for a while, the same magazine I brought from the city and have been reading over and over ever since. Behind me, Mauricio de Bernal keeps tapping the cage, coaxing the birds to come out. When the first bird swoops onto the back of the couch, tweeting with its lima bean lungs, I scream that I'm leaving. I yell for Yanina but get no response.

I walk outside, squeezing through the door quickly. Charlotte is sitting on a sewer drain playing cards by herself. Today she's wearing knee-length khaki shorts and a light blue tank top. I notice she has freckles on her shoulders.

"I'm going to the store," I say.

She collects the cards and slides them into her back pocket. "Can I go?" she asks. She speaks in English, with that accent of hers, and I do my best with my English in return.

"Do you like Panama?" I ask in the car on the way there.

She doesn't offer anything at first and then, "It's strange that there's no carpet here. And there are so many bugs."

"It's too hot for carpet."

"Yeah. It's, like, unbearably hot." She shakes her head as if she still can't get over that fact. She chews on a fingernail for a second and then picks herself up in the seat and plops back down to face me. "Have you ever seen the beetles outside at night? I'm just saying, there's millions of them. Last night it looked like all these thumbtacks rammed together over one whole side of the house."

"Thumbtacks?"

"Like little pins. You know, with heads?" When she sees I still don't understand, she says, "Forget it."

At the store we get some food and toilet paper. Charlotte is dismayed to find there's no chocolate to buy.

The woman at the counter has started a new scarf now, I see.

"You have a different woman," she says. Before I can respond she goes on, "My son is in New York. He claims everyone in the United States gets divorced. It's normal there. But a relationship should be sacred." She raises her eyebrows disapprovingly.

"She's just a friend," I say, pointing to Charlotte.

"Where is she from?" the woman asks.

"The United States."

"New York?"

"No," I say, though I realize I don't have a clue where she's from.

"Bah," the woman says, and wraps some yarn around her needles, like she has no use for anyone who's not from New York.

"Tennessee," Charlotte tells me on the way home, but I've never heard of it.

"Like tennis?" I ask.

She laughs. Her eyes crinkle at the corners when she does this and her teeth—big horse teeth—break free from behind her lips.

"Tennessee," she says again.

I shake my head.

"Have you heard of Elvis?" she wants to know.

"Don't step on my blue shoes!" I warble.

She laughs again and bites at her fingernail. "Blue *suede* shoes," she says. "Elvis is from Tennessee."

"Do you know Rubén Blades?" I ask.

She furrows her eyebrows. "Is he an actor?"

"A singer. From Panama."

"Is he good?"

"The best," I say, even though I never listen to him. But suddenly I want someone to be proud of, too.

When we reach the house, Mauricio de Bernal is on a chair in the bathtub, trying to grab one of the birds perched on the curtain rod. The bird keeps flying up and tapping down, like the curtain rod is a trampoline.

Yanina emerges from her room while I watch him. "Where have you been?" she asks.

"*Hola, mami!*" I say, and go to wrap her tiny body in my arms.

"Come, my love," Mauricio de Bernal's voice echoes.

Yanina tilts her face back. "All day like this!" She sighs, then drops her head against me again. "I missed you," she says into my chest.

"I went to the store."

"Why didn't you take me with you?"

"I couldn't find you." I pull my hand through the back of her hair.

She looks up suddenly. "Did you take Charlotte?"

I can't lie to her. I want to, but I can't. "Yes."

She takes two steps back. "Why?"

"She asked if she could come."

"How did she know you were going?"

"I was walking to the car and she saw me. Where else would I be going?"

She stands still and I can't decide if she's going to cry or hit me. But she doesn't do either. She looks at me with stony eyes, swallows hard, and then walks away without saying anything.

I could recite a list of all the times she's asked. In front of the lobster tank at Parrillada Jimmy; in a seminar room at the university; in the shoe section at Collins;

with yellow icing piped onto a sheet cake in the bakery; on street corners; in the parking lot of Wendy's; in the car; in love letters; so many places. By now, I think it's just a thing we have between us. I know she means it, but she has to understand that she has to wait for me. I've told her: I'm getting closer. I swear. Like it's a race where she's already crossed the finish line and I'm kilometers behind, struggling for air. There are days when I am positive, when I'm ready to ask her and just take off together. I look at her and think that there could be nothing better in this world than falling asleep next to her every night, our feet rubbing together under the sheet. But there are still those times, like pinpricks, that blow the air out of everything and I don't know again.

In the morning, Charlotte asks if I want to go for a walk. "We'll take the dogs," she announces, and goes to get them.

"René," she says as we walk. "That's a funny name. It's for a girl, you know."

"Here, it's for a boy."

Perro tugs on his leash and barks at something in the distance. He scrapes his paws on the ground, trying to run, but Charlotte keeps him on the dirt path. The sun is brutal, tearing into the earth. Delicate tangles of plants and flowers line the path, ones that Charlotte fingers as we walk by. At some point, Charlotte gets excited when she discovers a patch of *dormidera*.

"Why do they do that?" she asks when she touches one of the tiny green featherlike plants and it closes, pressing its fronds together tightly. She's peering at me from her crouch on the ground, shielding her eyes from the sun.

"They're scared. They don't like human contact."

"That can't be true," she murmurs.

I watch her, the curve of her back, her elbows sliding off her knees from sweat, pieces of her light hair matted to her burnt neck. She studies the fern with seriousness, holding her finger close to the stem to see if the leaves will close and then pulling it away again in frustration when they don't. I'm holding on to both Perro and Eva. They lie down, Eva thumping her tail against my toes.

When Charlotte finally stands, I can smell the odor lifting off her skin. Her skin is flushed.

"We call the plant *dormidera*," I say.

"*Dormidera*," she repeats softly. "That's nice."

We're standing face to face. Her skin is damp with sweat. Then she takes a step forward and kisses me. She does it with her mouth closed, just resting her lips on mine. On my skin, I can feel her breath pulsing gently. After a second, I pull away. Charlotte blinks. Her eyelids are the palest pink I've ever seen.

"I wanted to see what would happen," she says.

I don't say a thing. She purses her lips and casts her eyes around. I realize she thinks I didn't understand her and she's trying to come up with a different way to say it.

"What would happen," I repeat.

She focuses on me again, smiling. "You didn't close."

I let the words linger for a moment, stuck in the muggy air like needles in honey. I feel light-headed and suddenly aware that Eva's tail has stopped beating against my foot.

"We should go back," I say.

At the house, Yanina is in the kitchen making *arroz con pollo*. I watch her tearing the chicken meat into pieces with her hands. She seems surprised when we come in. I walk up and put my arms around her shoulders. I have this overpowering need to be near her. Now. Maybe always.

"What can I do?" I ask.

"You went out with Charlotte again?" She's trying to sound casual.

This time I lie. "I was on a walk. We happened to come into the house at the same time."

"I would have gone."

"I looked for you, *mami*."

"I need to get out of the house, too, you know. These stupid birds are making so much noise!" She flings a shred of meat against the counter.

It takes me a minute to realize she's crying. The fear that maybe she knows about the kiss between me and Charlotte sinks in.

From behind her, I smooth my whole hand over her face, trying to catch as many tears as I can. She kisses my palm as it passes her mouth. "I hate this," she says into my hand, and I realize she doesn't know after all. It's the house. It's the birds. It's being here. It's all of this.

Suddenly, one of the birds squawks loudly. Outside, Eva and Perro bark in return. Yanina screams, too, like it's an impromptu chorus.

When it grows quiet again, I say, "We have to leave."

"No," she says.

"Yanina, this is crazy. You know it is."

She shakes her head, but weakly.

"There's not enough room for us."

She turns and stares at me. "You told me. You said there is no such thing as a space in the world that one person can walk into and force another out."

"I'm sorry," I say. And I am, for the fact that I was wrong and for the fact that things operate like that—not enough space in the world, not enough space in a heart.

. . .

That night I sit on the patio, waiting for Yanina. Behind me the lights in the house are on, but in front of me is darkness. Mauricio de Bernal comes out and sits. It was a bad scene when he returned from church earlier and Yanina, tearfully, told him we were leaving. But he's calm now.

He's quiet for a while and then he says, "Yanina is full of love for you. She hopes you will become a husband to her."

I slide my hands under my thighs and sit on them.

"I want you to understand something about her parents. They were never married. That makes it easier for a man to leave. You know, of course, her father left. He found another woman. Lucia."

I didn't know her parents weren't married. Mauricio de Bernal grows quiet and focuses on something in the distance. A swarm of gnats, like a small web breathing in the air, comes together and then flies apart again.

He asks, "Do you know how her father died?"

"Yanina told me."

"The only reason for that job was to support the woman."

I think back to the story, that night in the car.

"I understand life does not work like that," he says. "God has crafted plans for us." He sighs. "But at times, in my head, I trace it back. If Carmen had married him in the first place, he might not have left. He might have felt bound to her. He might not have gotten that job. He might not have been on the bridge." He squints and steals a glimpse at the sky as he runs a hand through his hair. "It is very difficult to say."

Yanina walks out then, the screen door clattering behind her.

"You are ready?" Mauricio de Bernal asks, glancing up at her.

She bends to kiss him on the forehead and then rests her hand on my hair. "Let's go," she says, and we do.

We sleep on the beach that night. Who knows where we'll go next. The sand is damp and packed underneath us; the air gauzy, like pulled-apart cotton. I remember the last time we were here, with the crab legs, pale and pointy, the meat of some poking out at the breaks, and I think how long ago that seems now.

Yanina and I don't speak. We just lie on the sand in the dark, her head on my arm, our legs tangled. Her skin smells of coconut milk and I breathe her in as I listen to the static ocean sounds filling the world. I pull strands of her hair from the corner of her mouth when they lift in the breeze and get stuck there. After a while, when Yanina falls asleep, I get up. I can see only the edges of things, lit by the moon, and I walk for a few seconds, sweeping my feet along the ground, until I find a stick. I pick it up and then, cutting it through the sand, I write: YANINA, WILL YOU MARRY ME? I do the best I can in the dark, not sure whether the letters overlap and whether it will make sense in the light. I leave the stick there and find my way back to lie beside her. I think, if it's still there in the morning, if it hasn't been washed away, then that will mean something.

Then I will ask her.

ASHES

I'm at work on Saturday when I get the call. Carina, from the front counter, pages me over the intercom and when I finally get to the phone it's my older brother, Jano, advising me to sit down because he has upsetting news.

"Tell me," I say.

"Do you have a chair?"

"Just tell me."

What I have is a hollow feeling in my stomach the size of a coconut.

"Mamá's gone," he says.

"What?" My heart seizes.

"Señora López found her today."

"Found her? Where was Papi?"

"Are you sitting down?" he asks again.

"Stop asking me that. Why can't you just answer my questions?"

"It's a little bit complicated, okay?"

"How?"

But he won't answer that either. He just suggests we meet when I get off work because we have a lot of things to take care of now.

I'm not supposed to use the phone during work hours but I call Armando as soon as I hang up. I hold the plastic beige contraption trembling next to my ear as I talk. He tells me I should take off early, that my boss will understand because this is an extenuating circumstance. Armando's never had to work anywhere like this, though, and he doesn't get the idea that I'm just a body doing a job, not *somebody* doing it. Still, I tell him I'll try. He leaves me with, "We can go out for dinner if you want. You don't have to cook," like it's his big concession to me. "Thanks," I say, and slam down the phone.

I end up staying at Casa de la Carne for my whole shift. Work helps keep my mind off everything. If I'd left early, I would have been a blubbering thing sitting on the curb in the parking lot—the way I can be only in private, or sometimes, when he's being nice, with Armando. Never in front of my family. I know they think I'm more heartless than them for that, but I know the truth. I know my depths.

The story is that she had a heart attack. She was cooking—she was always cooking—and she simply fell over on the kitchen floor. Papi was sitting in a wooden chair at the kitchen table, probably smoking a cigarette while she worked, waiting to be served. She fell right at his feet. We think he tried to help her, tried to blow air into her mouth, pumping and puffing. Jano says Papi picked up the phone but he couldn't remember the number for emergency, and after trying a jumble of numbers over and over again, he just gave up.

"Why didn't he call one of us?" I say when I see Jano after work.

Jano shrugs. "I don't think he really knew what was happening."

We both know Papi is sick, mentally gone, but we never talk about him in those terms. We like to pretend he is just old.

When Señora López got there this morning, she found Papi still sitting in the wooden chair with the phone in his hand, buzzing because it was off the hook. She saw Mamá at his feet.

"The oven was still on, too," Jano says. "There could have been a fire on top of everything else." He shakes his head.

Señora López pried the phone from Papi's hands and called Jano.

"Papi's going to stay with me now," Jano says. "I don't think he can be alone."

"He can stay with me."

Jano shakes his head. "Uh-uh."

"Why not?"

"You have a newfound interest in him?"

"Do *you*?"

We're at an ice cream shop near my work. The cold air has turned Jano's lips faintly purple. Besides an employee in a pink apron, we're the only people here. The bright lights bounce off the white counters and smack me in the face. I'm quiet for a minute. Then I start on a reel of questions. How does he know it was a heart attack? What are we going to do now? What's happening to their house? Is his wife, Zenia, okay with Papi being there? What else did Papi say? Why did Señora López call him instead of me?

He answers them all. He's unusually patient with me. He's waiting to see if I'll break, I know, if this will be the thing that puts me over the edge.

．　．　．

The last time I saw her, my mother was sitting with me on her patio. She was in the metal rocking chair we had my whole life, olive-green seat cushions and floral iron-work along the arms. She had her legs stretched out in front of her, knee-high nylons rolled down around her crossed ankles like life preservers, terry house slippers on her feet. She looked relaxed as she lectured me on her favorite subject—politics. She was telling me how fortunate it was that she had named me Mireya because the president of Panama was Mireya Moscoso. She must have said about ten times, "That could have been you," as if the only prerequisite for becoming the president was having the right name.

She hated that politics held no interest for me. The one thing my mother liked about Armando was his appetite for the political. Just for that, of all the people in my family, she was his only fan.

That day, there was an election parade in the neighborhood. Martín Torrijos was riding all over our section of town, shouting from the windows of his van and waving a Panamanian flag in a bid to become the next president. This was the reason we were out on the patio. My mother was waiting for him. We'd been talking for almost an hour when his big white van, followed by pickup trucks with speakers on the flatbeds blasting music, rumbled up our street. My mother stood and smoothed out the front of her robe. She was old enough that her spine had begun to bow.

Torrijos stopped his van in front of our patio. He asked my mother how she and her sister, meaning me, were doing.

My mother shouted, "What will you do about the hospitals?"

Torrijos smiled and waved.

"And what about the canal?" she yelled into the sunlight.

Torrijos tossed a T-shirt out the window to her. "For you!" he shouted.

My mother let it land at her feet. "*Pendejo!*" she shouted, and the van continued up the street.

It wasn't everyone who would call a politician an asshole to his face. I smiled until it felt like my cheeks would burst. I'd always thought there was something special between my mother and me. Like she was somehow more mine than Jano's. But maybe all children feel that—a sovereignty of ownership over the parent they love best.

On the bus home from work that night, I pass strip malls with blinking neon signs; a place where there was once a major bust of Noriega supporters and where now a guy tries to sell Oriental rugs; billboards that advertise electronics and lingerie; high-rise concrete apartment buildings with laundry strung on every balcony; roadside stands with vendors selling fruit, the pineapples hanging from columns of rope attached to the stands' roofs like beaded curtains; an older man holding a wire birdcage, being trailed as he walks down the street by an obviously American girl.

When I get home Armando sprints out to see me.

"*Pobrecita*," he says. He's making a face like I'm a puppy with a broken leg. "I have a poem for you."

"Another one?"

"When was the last one?" he asks, leaning over the kitchen table, reaching for a book. He finds the page he wants and says, "It's by César Vallejo. He's one of the great writers. He wrote for the people."

I sit down as he reads it to me. I don't understand poetry the way he does. Things either sound good to me or they don't. That's it. The poem he reads tonight is short. It's about the poet's brother, who died. My favorite line is: "And now a shadow falls on the soul." I feel the tears burn behind my eyes.

"It's nice," I say when he's done. Then I quickly scoot my chair back and head straight for the shower. Under the spray, the meat juices wash from my fingernails, from my pores. I tilt my head back and let the water stream down my face until I can't tell anymore where the water ends and my tears begin.

Armando comes in after me. He knows this is my place to cry. He peels off his clothes and steps into the stall and tries to hold me. His dark, moppish hair sticks to the sides of his face. His skin slips over mine. He pushes me out of the water and examines my eyes. "Are the tears gone now?"

I shrug.

"Tell me, Mireya," he pleads. It's that split second of something in his voice that, despite everything else, makes me love him.

"I think they're just starting," I say.

He bends down and licks one cheek, then the other, gently, with the tip of his tongue. "I'll get them," he says, and he does.

My father cleaned government buildings at night. He came home in the early morning hours, high on ammonia and bleach, and made my mother prepare dinner for him in the dark. When he worked overtime, she cooked dinner while the sun rose. Many nights the smell of spicy chicken or *ropa vieja* woke me up and I knew that my father had just arrived. During the day, he should have been sleeping, but more often he was out in bars or with other women or smoking on our front step, ashes fluttering in the air like confetti. My mother was never happy with him. I mean, she must have been at one time, but I never witnessed it. I'd hear her, at night, through our thin walls, sobbing in her room.

She knew what my father did—I often heard them arguing about his carryings on—but, for all her strength, she was never able to change him and never able to walk away. There was one time when I thought she came close. My father had taken a job cleaning houses during the day and at some point he started returning home with hair dryers, mixing bowls, toaster ovens, picture frames. Of course, we knew where these things were coming from. No one said anything, though, until a police officer showed up at our house one afternoon asking questions. It was easy enough to get rid of him—my father offered him a speaker system—but I'd never, until that moment, seen my mother so angry. For a whole week, she spoke to him only once, when she told him, "You shamed me."

The only time I saw a moment of affection between them was much later, after Jano had married and I had moved out on my own. My father had retired and they were living off his pension and the odd lottery payout. My mother had asked me to get some melons for her at the stand near my house and bring them over. She was very particular about which melons she deemed acceptable. When I got there the front door was wide open and I saw my parents inside, sitting on our old peach-colored couch, my father at one end, and my mother stretched out at the other, her feet propped on his lap. He was tickling the soles of her feet with his fingertips and she was flinching, but laughing. Then he reached over and tucked her hair behind her ear. She followed the movement of his hand with her head, like a horse. That was all. But there was real tenderness in it.

Armando is Argentinean, a different breed. We met six months ago when I was on my way out of work one afternoon, heading for the bus. He must have been standing there for hours, surveying every so-and-so who walked by. I'm not beautiful. I know that. I'm just this girl with my mother's squash-shaped body, and dense black hair and a mole on my right cheek. But I always thought it meant something that he seized on me. Came right up to me and said, "You look like you could use a decent meal. Can I take you out?" He had on brown slacks and a white linen shirt. I brushed him off at first.

"What's your name?" he asked.

"Mireya."

He stopped in his tracks, playing. "That's perfect," he said. "The reservation is under Mireya."

It was such a line. But I liked the idea of going someplace where we would need a reservation so I said yes.

We ended up at one of the best steakhouses in Panama City, a spot with gold doors that have an image of a bull carved into them. It was the first and last time we ever went out to a dinner like that. He paid for the whole thing and I ate a lot, as much as I could get in me. At the end of the meal he asked if he could sleep on my floor for a few nights. Told me that he'd just arrived in Panama and didn't know anyone and he didn't want to go back to Argentina because of some issue with his parents. I found out later it was money—his wealthy parents had finally told him he needed to find a job or get out. The idea of a job was distasteful to a person like Armando so he got out. He said he would pay me for a place on the floor, but he never did. And he promised to keep his hands to himself, but he didn't do that either. But he seemed harmless enough at the time. So there, in the steakhouse, my belly warm and full, I said yes.

Carina, at work, says I only fell for him out of habit. The habit of seeing him every day. She says, "Imagine someone put a plate with a nice big pork chop on it in front of you. But you felt like a hamburger so you said no thanks. And then the next day they brought you a plate with the same big pork chop. And the next day and the next day. Eventually you would start wanting it, even though in the beginning you had no interest. Right?"

"Armando's not a pork chop," I say.

She shrugs. "At least a pork chop would feed you."

Two days pass and I still can't get myself together. It's like a small, ferocious animal pounces on me every day, clawing at me, tearing me to shreds. I go outside on my break and sit on the concrete step behind Casa de la Carne by myself. The ground is slick with grease, and mangy dogs sniff around my feet but I'm too ruined to care. When my time is over, I mop up my face and reassemble my hair into a ponytail.

I can't stop thinking about the fact that my mother's gone, though. It's bad. I cut my finger twice on the slicer before lunchtime has even rolled around. When I tell them I don't care and that I don't want to wear the steel-mesh safety gloves while I cut, they send me home.

Armando's on his back on the couch, his socked feet up on the arm, reading. The whole place smells like sweat from his socks.

"What are you doing here?" he asks, startled, when I come in.

"They sent me home."

"You were fired?" He looks terrified.

For a second, I have this impulse to answer yes, to tell

him he's the one who has to find a job now, figure out a way to support us both, just to see what he would do.

I shrug. "They just sent me home."

He purses his lips and looks away, like he's weighing what this might mean.

"What? You have someone coming over?" I ask.

"No."

He cheated on me once, when we first started, with this girl who had air-conditioning at her place. He told me it was because he liked to sleep there—no mosquitoes, no night sweats. He claimed it had nothing to do with her, but there were a few nights even during a blackout when he went over there, just the same. So. He might have left me for her at some point, I don't know, but she moved to the United States anyway.

"I'm trying to finish this book by tomorrow," he says, holding up what's in his hand. "You won't bother me, right?"

"I'm going to make lunch." I raise my fingers to show him the bandages, but he's already back to his book.

"Meatballs and *patacones* for me?" he asks hopefully. "Oh, and your papi called. I think it was him. He said it was him at first and then he kept saying he had the wrong number. The man is messed up, Mireya. You guys should put him in a hospital, you know?"

I glare at him as he reads. I unwrap the tape and

gauze—pink with my blood—from my fingers, balancing them in my hand, and consider throwing them at him. But I don't. I just leave them at his feet to see if he'll even notice.

I call my father back later that night. Zenia answers. She's never liked me. I think that when she and Jano first started together years ago, he told her not to trust me. My brother has always suffered from the belief that I came into the world to steal my parents' attention from him. When I was younger, he claimed that for the entire ride to the hospital while my mother was in labor with me, she had shouted, "I don't want it!" "You see?" he said. "Even then she knew you were a bad idea." My mother heard him and swatted him on the arm so hard that a patch of red bloomed on his skin.

"Is my father there?" I ask.

"He's having a good time here, you know."

"Please, Zenia. I want to talk to him."

She sighs. "*Momentito.*"

"*Aló?*" he says when he gets on the phone. "Who is this?"

"It's Mireya."

"*La presidenta?*"

"No. It's me. Your daughter."

It sounds like he's chewing on something.

"How are you doing?" I ask.

"Fine. There's a fan in my bedroom," he says.

"What are you eating?"

"I'm drinking."

"You're chewing your drink?"

He's quiet.

"Are you okay over there? Are you happy?"

"I miss you," he says, and it's so unexpected. I wonder if he even knows who he's talking to.

"Me?"

"That fan makes a lot of noise, though."

"I'll tell Jano to fix it for you."

"I used to live in my own house. Is that right?"

"Yes."

He's silent again.

"Do you want me to come visit you?" I ask.

My father was drunk almost every day while I was
growing up. He was hardly around, a shadow of a father.
It's no secret that Jano and I hardened ourselves to him.
But still, it's amazing how much I want him to say yes.

"Our dinner is ready," he says instead.

"Okay, Papi."

"We're having *arroz con pollo*."

"I'm going to get off now. I'll see you in a few days."

"Yes. It would be very nice to see the president."

"Good-bye, Papi."

. . .

When I show up at Casa de la Carne the next day, Carina pulls me aside and asks what I'm doing there. "I thought you got fired," she says. I assure her I was just sent home early because of personal problems. She shakes her head at me, her gold hoop earrings swaying against her jaw. "No," she says, drawing it out as if the word were a rubber band. "I think you should talk to Tino." But as soon as she says it, I understand. I didn't wear the gloves, which is a safety violation, which is a big deal. I was an idiot to think that they were just giving me some time off to pull myself together. Tino confirms it.

I don't go home right away, though. I take the bus to my parents' house. It's on a sloping street where the houses press against one another, side by side, like children in a line holding hands. Theirs looks like all the others: a big cement patio out front, bars over the windows, wire trash bins held up on poles by the curb. I open the gate and step onto the patio. For some reason I'm feeling nervous, like I'm trespassing. Even so, I'm doing okay until I notice the chair where I last saw my mother. The seat cushion is still flattened from her weight, the imprint of her bottom a depression in the foam. It splits my heart in two. I take a few deep breaths and make my way to the chair. Slowly, I lower myself into the impression she formed. The air is blistering, the sun piercing. I sit for as long as I can take it, and then I have to leave.

Memories are thin, watery and fragile like gas rising off the pavement on the hottest days. But there are times I can see clearly.

I was eight. We had driven to my Tía Cre's house for a party. The boys abandoned us, locking themselves in a room doing who knows what, but no one asked because they were boys and anything was permissible. My cousin Juanita and I went down to the spiny shores of the bay, rooting around for snails and crabs in the small pools that gathered between the rocks. This was my mother's favorite place. She was forever reminiscing about growing up in a house on the bay, about the days when she and Tía Cre spent their time among the rocks and on the crescent of sand at their base.

Juanita and I were barefoot, and the ocean rolled in far enough at times to lick the rocks until they glistened. I was stepping down from one rock to another when I slipped. My feet shot out in front of me and I fell backward. My spine hit the rock and my head snapped against a rough crest of stone. I must have blacked out for a few seconds. When I was conscious again, I reached up and felt the blood sticky in my hair.

I had a gash like a long slug, just behind my ear. My cousin ran screaming to the house. I don't remember much between then and when my mother arrived.

I saw her bending over me. I saw the sunlight filtering through her black hair, which curled under at the tips. There was a look of consternation on her face; she looked like she wanted to slap me but couldn't bring herself to do it. She had a white apron around her waist—she must have been helping my Tía Cre in the kitchen—and I remember it flapping over me as she leaned down and scooped me up.

The blood stopped soon enough. My Tía Cre cleaned and bandaged me. The adults were worried and then not worried. My father looked at me blandly—he was drunk—and declared that I would be fine. Jano came out of the bedroom with a joystick in his hand, the cord stretching all the way across the floor. He peered at me and then walked away, shrugging. I think he thought I was just creating a show to get attention. To prove him wrong, I bit my lip to keep from crying. I haven't cried in front of my family since.

In my cousin's dark bedroom, the windows wide open and the curtains blowing, my mother stayed with me while the party went on. She climbed into bed and held me from behind.

"I'm not happy," she said.

"I didn't mean to do it," I told her. My head throbbed.

"You aren't allowed to leave me, you know."

I could smell the vegetable oil and cooking gas that had crept into the fabric of her clothes and her hair.

"Everyone else can leave, but not you."

My head stung, pain pulsing around me like a halo. I heard the muffled sounds of the party through the door—ice clinking into glasses, spontaneous riots of laughter, a faint thread of music. "I'm sorry," I said.

She sighed and then pinched a bit of skin on my arm and twisted it. I knew then that she really *had* wanted to hit me back on the rocks. The pinch was a compromise.

"Be more careful," she said. "From now on, you do that for me."

The day before the funeral, I'm cruising around town on the bus. There's not much else to do. Everyone still thinks I have a job so I have to leave the house during the day.

The bus is maybe a kilometer out when, through the window, I see Armando. From the back, but I can tell it's him. He's walking with his arm around a girl's shoulder, her arm around his waist. She's taller than me and her wrist is dripping with jewelry, expensive-looking stuff, the kind you could only get at a place like Mercurio. I get off at the next stop and walk back toward them.

I'm about ten meters away when Armando sees me. He drops his arm from the woman's shoulder. "You're not at work," he says when I'm close enough.

"I don't work there anymore."

The woman next to him is wearing big, round sunglasses that are probably designer.

"What do you mean?"

"I just don't." I stare unblinkingly at the woman as I say it. I can't see her eyes, but I can see her eyebrows lift behind her sunglasses.

"Hey," he says. It's that soft "Hey" he gives me sometimes in the middle of the night when he wants to wake me because, he says, he misses me. He takes me by the arm and drags me a few steps away.

"Is that the same girl from before?" I ask. As soon as I say it, though, I realize I don't want the answer. Either way, it's bad.

He shakes his head.

"Who is she, then?"

"Mireya, please."

"How long have you been with her?" I ask.

He shakes his head again.

"Tell me how long!"

"A few weeks, okay?"

"She's rich?"

"She gives me what I need." He looks defiant, suddenly. He's over his shame or he's pretending to be over it.

"I don't? I go to work so you can eat!"

"Armando," the woman calls.

That's when I lay into him. Just sock him one in the chest. He stumbles back and the next thing I know I'm lunging at him, tearing into his pockets, grabbing hold of what I can. He clutches my wrists, trying to pry my hands away. But I want it—whatever he has, I want it. With both of us pulling, the seam of his pocket rips and he starts yelling at me to stop, but I won't. He rams the top of his head against my shoulder, trying to create some distance between us. And somehow we end up on the ground, tiny pebbles pressing into my skin, the sidewalk baking underneath us. Faintly, I hear the woman saying "*Ay, Dios,*" again and again, and I catch glimpses of her towering over us as we fight. Finally, Armando manages to pull free of me and stand. I get up, too, and brush myself off.

The woman says, "Armando, this girl is crazy."

I'm a firestorm inside—everything exploding and burning—and I'm trying so hard not to talk because I know if I do, I'll cry.

Armando tells the woman to wait at the corner. You can tell she's not used to being instructed to do anything, especially not by him. But she does it.

It doesn't help that eventually I would have left him anyway, or that anyone could have seen this coming.

We stare at each other, squinting in the sun. His face is light—he's always been too pale for this country—and shiny with sweat. I can't help thinking that there were moments when he was good to me. I wait for him to say something but he doesn't. I feel weightless standing there, like I'm not sure if the soles of my shoes are connected to the sidewalk anymore.

"My mother was the only one in my family who liked you," I finally say. It's a petty impulse—wanting to hurt him because he hurt me—but I don't care.

He looks like I just slapped him. "Your mother?"

I grab my bag from the ground and start walking away. I hear his shoes shuffle behind me for a second and then stop.

"What about you?" he yells. "Didn't you like me?"

It's such a heartbreaker. Because here's the answer: Yes, I did. Who knows why, but I did.

The funeral is what it is. I kiss a hundred cheeks and listen to a hundred stories about what a wonderful person my mother was. Everyone's asking where Armando is but I say again and again that I don't want to get into it. Jano ran an obituary in the newspaper. He looks terrible, his nose red, his eyes swollen like little ravioli. Zenia, in a long-sleeved white dress, never leaves his side, her arm hooked through his. My father is seated in the front pew and I wave to him because I'm not sure what he would think if I hugged him.

When the time comes, I go up to say good-bye to her. When my grandmother died, I remember walking up the church aisle, gripping my mother's hand. I was five. In my memory, the other people in the church are blurry, only watercolors. When my mother and I got to the casket, I could see my grandmother's face—powdery and calm. I wanted so badly to touch her; I stood there forever thinking about doing it, but I didn't think I was allowed. I didn't want to do it and cause a scene, one that Jano would chide me for later. That afternoon I asked my mother if I could have done it. She told me of course. For all these years, I've hated the fact that I didn't.

Now there's no casket, just a gold urn on a small table. What can I do, reach my hand in? A photograph of my mother sits on an easel next to the urn. It's black-and-white, all soft edges and haze. She is too young for me to recognize her. I wonder, if I hadn't been her daughter, if I had just met this woman in the photograph on the street, would I have liked her? But it's a stupid thing to wonder, because of course I would have. I would have loved her anytime.

When I'm done, I take a seat beside Papi. He smiles. His long, thin fingers are folded in his lap, and he looks as light and unbothered as a cloud.

"How are you?" I ask. I feel none of the anger I usually do around him.

"I tried to save her," he whispers, leaning sideways.

"I know, Papi," I say.

"Human beings can't save each other from anything, though."

"I'm sorry," I tell him, because I don't know what else there is to offer.

He nods. "Nothing to be sorry about."

"Okay," I say, and he pats my knee.

Afterward, I take the urn with me. Jano has already said, without any discussion, that he will keep it at his house, but in my mind it's inconceivable that it could belong to anyone but me.

Holding the urn in my lap, I take a taxi straight to the bay, passing billboards and wire fences, fields of overgrown grass freckled with tiny flowers and small fires, ramshackle houses and brittle palm trees.

When we get to the bay, I pay the driver. He has a stern face and he simply nods before shooting off into the gathering darkness. I carry the urn to the rocks and sit down, balancing it beside me. I take off the lid and reach my hand in, letting my fingertips graze the dust. Then I cover it again. I sit there for hours, my bottom growing damp from the glaze of water clinging to the rocks, and look out for anything I can see.

DRIVE

1.

In my dream, we are driving so fast the car sprouts wings—giant, bony, feather-covered wings—and we are flying like gulls, steady, just above the glossy surface of the pavement. Everyone is laughing bubbles and confetti and the wind laces its fingers through our hair and streams it back and we can't feel the cool air against our faces because it is so gentle that it cannot be felt.

But when I tell Beto about my dream he laughs and says it's finally official: I am one seriously fucked *chica*.

I go to slap his arm but he grabs my wrist before I

even come close. He looks me in the eye, little glints of green sparkling at me, all playful, and says, "But you're still *my chica*, you know. You're always mine." He's grinning so it lights up his face like he's in a contest with the sun and I can't help but stroke his sideburns with my free hand and smile back. I start tripping kisses down his neck until he picks me up and takes me to the bed where we stay, trying to get closer, in each other's skin, all afternoon.

2.

I work at Mattito's, trying to talk anyone who will listen into buying a dishwasher or a blender or a new television. There's one other girl, Yanina, in my department, but we work different shifts. I've been here for two years; before this I was mowing the grass in a cemetery and getting eaten alive by mosquitoes and burnt by the sun, so this was a step up. Still, it's not great. The way I see it, appliances are a hard sell in a country where most people fill a plastic tub with soapy water and wash their dishes by hand or string their clothes out on a line to dry, and those who don't, have maids to do these things for them. To my boss, Señor Contreras, though, all of this means Panama is the perfect market for appliances because he thinks the only reason people do things by hand is that they don't realize there's an easier way, and that's where I'm supposed to come in.

Mattito's is in a strip mall on a busy street, two lanes both ways with aluminum pedestrian bridges at every corner to deliver people safely from side to side. Buses and trucks and black taxicabs and motorcycles roar past at all hours, honking and swerving through traffic. On one side of us is a beauty salon that does way more business than we ever will, and on the other side is a guy who sells rugs out of a storefront that used to be a popular restaurant until the owner was reported to have ties to Noriega and the whole thing was wiped clean by American soldiers.

I'm walking around, straightening the price tags on the dryers, when Beto calls me on his cell to tell me he's scored some premium stuff. His supplier gave him a tiny bag like some kind of year-end bonus.

"*Oye*, I'm at work," I whisper into the phone.

"Then don't be at work," Beto says.

3.

I meet him at his apartment above a lingerie store on Avenida Central and I thank God for the millionth time that I know at least one person in this city who doesn't still live with his parents. The mannequins in the window of the shop are a mess, wigs sliding off their bald heads, bras ill-fitting around their plastic breasts. Beto has names for them—Yasmine and Josefina—and whenever we walk by he waves to them or asks them how things are going today or compliments them on maintaining such nice figures, so I kind of think of them as real and I smile at them before I head upstairs.

Beto's sitting on the floor reading the newspaper when I come in. Or else he's pretending to read it, which is something he does sometimes so people will think he's smart when in reality he's just looking at the ads for the department stores to see the models in their big underwear like bags up to their ribs. *Viejo* underwear, but he thinks it's kind of hot.

"I knew you'd show," he says after I walk over to him and kiss him on the head. He wraps his arms around my calves so that my knees buckle and I nearly fall on top of him.

"Only for an hour," I tell him.

"Bah." He nuzzles his face into my thighs and then pulls back. "I had a dream," he says, looking up at me. "Those washing machines grew legs and walked out of the store themselves and then they grew arms and knocked on peoples' doors and begged for homes and the people asked where they were from and the *máquinas* told them Mattito's and the people said, 'I will keep you and tomorrow I will take my money to Mattito's and pay for you,' and the washing machines were happy because now they were sold and they knew that meant you, who was their favorite person, would get a nice raise and you wouldn't have to go back to work all day." He laughs and how I love the sound of that laugh like a spring bubbling out through his mouth.

"Now who's fucking *loco* for real?" I say, steadying myself with my knees against his shoulder and running my fingertips along the strands of his bristly dark hair.

4.

When I get home that night, my mamá's snoring on the couch. She has a body like a big yam—everything fleshy and sweet—and I stand over her, trying to imagine how my own body will turn into that one day. She tells me it's going to happen, that eventually I'm going to blow up and fill out into a shape like her, but I think that's only if I have kids, which I'm not planning on doing. Beto and I have already talked about it.

My mamá had four kids. Two died before they were even a few weeks in this world, another is a girl, gone off to who knows where but I never knew her, and the fourth one is me. My papi's in the city, in some ghetto barrio somewhere. I see him out sometimes but he never gets around to acting like my father so I've finally learned to stop trying to act like his daughter. The last time I saw him was at a restaurant where Beto and I went for chicken. He was at the bar watching a horse race on TV. He nodded and gave a wave when he saw us but it was in a way that made me know he didn't want me to come over or anything. He was with some other *hombres.* So the whole night Beto and I sat out on the patio eating our chicken and I watched my papi's back through the window and tried to will myself into thinking of him as just any old man with a skinny hunch and a chin pointy as a spade and graying hair. Beto kept saying the whole situation was shit. But really, I told him, it wasn't so bad. There are two ways you can go in this life: Either a whole family, twenty people or whatever, stick together and live all in one house like a big pod, or else everyone's spread all over, like seeds, and you each replant yourself and make a new life on your own. One's not better than the other, I don't think, but they each require certain adjustments.

5.

Señor Contreras informs me that we haven't sold a single appliance in seventeen days. The executives at the department store headquarters are getting nervous and making threats about getting rid of the appliances department in our location.

"Is it really just us?" I ask.

He's a roly-poly man with greasy hair combed straight

back. The only clothes I've ever seen him wear are a tan suit paired with a lemon-yellow shirt, and I wonder sometimes whether he squeezed out of his mother in that suit and whether he will die in it. I can tell he wants to answer yes because he thinks that might scare me into working harder. But finally he sighs and shakes his head.

"No person wants to buy appliances," he says, as if he were the one who invented appliances and is taking it as a personal affront.

It's like this all over the city. People don't want to change or else they can't afford it. A few months ago two new highways opened here. The south highway runs through the city and is supposed to ease up traffic everywhere else except that it doesn't go exactly where anyone needs it to and it costs up to $3.00 to use it. Who's going to pay to drive on a stupid highway when the other roads are free? The north highway costs the same and was built mostly to connect the airport to the city, so it was pretty obvious from the beginning that it was mainly for the tourists. To us, that highway was a rejection. On the old route, visitors would have seen the billboards for Café Durán and Daewoo and Adidas and they would have seen people with umbrellas at bus stops and walking the streets with shopping carts. They would have seen stray dogs darting like tadpoles over broken streets and unpaved shoulders overgrown with plants. They would have heard corrugated metal gates grinding down at the end of the day and horns bleating their impatience and men whooping at the women walking by. They would have seen real life here. But I guess real life is often unsightly, so they built a highway straight into the heart of the city to keep tourists away from what's real, away from the heart of us.

The speed limit on both highways is an insane eighty kilometers an hour, a speed unheard of in a country where being in a car either means being mired in a sea of traffic or navigating small dirt roads. The very thought of shooting around in a car that fast scares the shit out of everyone.

The highways and appliances, they're all very modern, you know. And they go basically unused.

6.

When I was seven my papi took me out driving. We were in El Rompío, where the dark green plants on the side of the road swayed over us like ballerina arms, and he put me on his lap in the driver's seat and let me steer the car down a dusty stretch while he worked the pedals. I remember it so well because that was the last time I touched him. My whole self was right up on him and his arms were around my waist and I could feel his breath against my ear when he told me to turn more or to hold on tighter. He had this aftershave that smelled like cinnamon milk, and for a long time after that I went to drugstores all over the city, twisting caps off aftershave bottles, trying to find that smell again. My mother was back at a roadside bodega. I knew she was probably standing there wringing her hands, praying that we didn't crash or drive off straight into the sea. And I loved that feeling—my papi and me together like *bandidos*, bumping over the gravel in the scorching midday sun, shredding the earth beneath us as we went. Most memories might be like water, but some are like wood—so solidly there that you can feel them and smell them and wrap your hands around them, and for a hundred years they will never go away.

7.

I spend a long time getting ready in the morning. I'm the kind of girl who walks down the street trying to get stared at as much as possible without actually being whistled at. Beto's all, Why do you care, Marisol? You want me to whistle at you? I'll whistle at you until your fucking ears fall off your fucking head. And even though I can see his point and I'm for real not trying to pick up other guys, I just think it might be nice if I could. Anyway, my mamá, who doesn't much like Beto since he has no job to speak of and since he doesn't live with his family—which she says shows a lot of nerve and disrespect—she's the one always buying me lipsticks and eyeshadows from the Supermarket Rey and leaving them on my bed. She gets seriously wrapped up in those commercials that advertise a product that will give you perfect skin or lashes that extend all the way to the moon. "You're so young," she says. "You have to take advantage before you turn into an old woman."

"You still look good," I tell her but she sweeps away the words with her hand.

"You still have time to get a man," she says.

"I have one."

"You have a *cabrón*."

"Mamá!" I wail.

We get in this fight all the time. And whenever we do, it sends me straight to Beto.

8.

We've got a customer walking around in braided Italian loafers, his arms crossed. He's looking very earnestly at one of our top-of-the-line refrigerators. It's got an ice maker, which is really the big selling point because ice is essential in all this Panamanian heat and at every party you have to buy big bags of it and bang them against the floor until the ice inside crumbles into little cubes that you can slide into your guests' glasses. An ice maker would be a real savior to someone who could afford it.

Señor Contreras is perched in a loftlike area above the store where he's always sorting things like receipts and inventory sheets. There are tilted mirrors all around the store so that from where he stands, he can see what's going on at any moment. He's looking down at me now like he's about to start throwing things if I don't pounce on this customer soon, so I walk over casually and ask if the guy needs help with anything.

"How much do you charge for delivery?" he asks, and I have a hard time swallowing for a second because if he's asking about delivery already, this is serious.

"Twenty-five dollars," I tell him and he nods.

There's some more back and forth on the details—I dutifully point out the ice maker—and eventually he's ready to sign for a new refrigerator. It's almost too easy.

And then, because I'm on some kind of real high about it, I suggest that maybe he wants to look at a new dryer. I don't know anyone on the planet who actually owns a dryer but I'm feeling like maybe today is my lucky day so why not ride it out?

The guy smirks at me and says, "Ever heard of the sun?"

He starts laughing and I pray to God that to Señor Contreras it looks like we're having a good time down here.

"I just thought—" I start.

"You know what? Forget all of it," he says. "I don't need a new refrigerator like I don't need a dryer."

And that's it. He's headed for the door. I follow him a few steps and even call out, Señor, Señor, but he's ignoring me, so I just try to act casual and wave to his back as he's leaving. There's no getting around the fact that I fucked up, though. That sale would have been two months' rent. But he's gone.

9.

That night Beto and I make it good. It's impossibly hot in his apartment so we decide to take a cold shower together. We try a little in the stall but we keep slipping and not being able to find a good spot so eventually we get out, still streaming wet, and go to the bed. Beto runs on his toes to the other room to get the fan. When he plugs it in he aims it toward us and sets it on high. I have this image of beads of water scampering over my skin. They lose their shape and splay out over my shoulders and my back and my calves, trying to outrun the wind. In their wake, they leave me covered with goosebumps and it's this combination—Beto's fingers stroking between my thighs and the sharp coolness pricking at my skin—that sends me over in a way I've never experienced before.

Afterward, we're lying on the damp sheet and staring at the stucco ceiling together. The best thing about Beto's apartment, besides the fact that it's his, is that the streets around here have all been made into pedestrian walkways so it stays close to quiet most of the time. Tonight is no exception. We lie there for so long without speaking or moving that I wonder if Beto has fallen asleep. He often does and I always cover him with a sheet so that the mosquitoes don't get to him in the night, and then I kiss him and leave quietly because my mamá doesn't let me stay over. But now I turn my head just in time to see his hand, which has been resting on his chest, move as he raises his fingers to his nose.

"What are you doing?" I ask.

"I can smell you," he says. He holds his fingers there and breathes in, closing his eyes and smiling, until finally his hand drops away.

10.

Sometimes, at night, I go out walking. This is long after the neon signs throughout the city have blinked out, but before the *panaderías* start their lonely business of rolling dough in the early half-light of morning. No one knows I go, or maybe they do and they don't mention it, but I do it because it's the time when I feel the most alone in the world but it's also the time when I feel most intimately connected to it. Like the hour confers some kind of clarity of vision in which everything appears to me in its true, naked state, and everything in this city makes sense to me, at least for a little while.

I'm just past a church when I see my father. He's sitting on the arm of a bench, breaking seeds with his teeth and eating whatever's inside. A plastic bag hangs from one wrist. It's the strangest feeling whenever I see him—like seeing the love of your life, the one who left you, when you're just out doing errands, trying to keep up with the business of the everyday. You half want to run and jump on them and bury your face in their neck and hold on forever and you half want to turn away, shielding yourself.

I'm about to walk closer when he sees me and yells out, "*Tienes plata para un viejo?*"

I wonder if he's drunk.

He yells out, please, any money I can spare, and we're staring at each other under the moon but to him I'm just anybody.

I turn around finally and walk back the way I came.

11.

A few more weeks and Señor Contreras tells me it's over. I'm secretly relieved to hear this because it means no more tirelessly pushing things on people that they don't really need.

"Can I be moved to cosmetics?" I ask. I'm thinking how much my mamá would love that because I'd probably get a good discount, but Señor Contreras is staring at me with his small eyes and it's then I know I'm not getting it. It's not just that I'm being transferred to another department or something. I feel like my head's made out of cement when I realize what's happening.

"I'm sorry, Marisol," he says, but he's not really and both of us know it. "It's a bad time," he tells me. When I don't respond, he adds, "I had to let Yanina go, too."

I nod.

"*Buena suerte,*" he says finally, and that's it.

12.

Beto's trying to tell me it's no big deal.

"You'll get something else," he says. He's stoned and glassy, like a gigantic talking marble, and he warbles on and on about how I was better than that job and about how Señor Contreras is a fucking *payaso* and whatever. He has a joint rolled for me already and he pinches the tip again before lighting it and handing it to me. I take it between my fingers and put it to my lips and inhale, holding the smoke in my lungs while he blathers on.

Finally I let the smoke go and feel a rush of warmth to my head. I tell him I don't want to discuss it anymore.

A bowl of stale gumdrops sits on the coffee table and from where he lies on the couch, Beto drops his hand in like a crane and starts rifling through them.

We smoke a little more and after a while, I say, "Did I tell you I saw my papi the other night?"

"You shouldn't call him that," he cautions. "You should call him by his first name, you know."

"He asked me for money."

"Jesus. And did you tell him to fuck off?"

I don't say anything at first. I look around the room at the plastic furniture and the white bars outside the windows and the gold refrigerator humming in the kitchen. Beto's got a few plants on the sill but one of them is dying. He gets really pissed about it, too.

"How's your baby plant?" I ask. Beto pulls his hand out of the gumdrops and shakes the sugar from his fingertips. I watch the granules shower to the floor.

"Whatever," he says, and leans his head back against the couch, the plastic squeaking underneath him.

13.

When I get home, my mamá is watching *Sábado Gigante* in her nightgown. The television is doing a light show on her face. As soon as she sees me she gets up and puts her hands on my shoulders.

"What happened to you?" she asks. Her mascara is oily under her eyes and her hair is flat against the back of her head where she's been resting it.

"How do you know?" I say, although she always knows. She has crazy intuitions.

She looks at me sadly. "Mari," she says.

"Señor Contreras said he was sorry, though," I tell her. "I'll find a new job soon."

She shakes her head. "There's something else, *hija*." I wonder for a second if she can tell I'm high and I concentrate to make sure it seems like I'm on earth while I'm talking to her but then she drops her hands to my stomach and holds them there. "It's in here," she whispers.

She looks at me and shakes her head and sighs.

14.

There's no way I'm going to tell Beto. I'm going to lose it as easily as it came. My mamá thinks I'm wrong on both counts. She stopped talking to me as soon as I said it. I would come to the kitchen table in the morning to have some bread and some *piña*, and I tried: How did you sleep last night, Mamá? What are you doing today? Do you want me to get you anything at the store? But she moved around, clearing the dishes from the table, rolling the top of the brown paper bag closed so that the bread would stay fresh, acting as though I didn't exist.

I broke a plate once. I had just pulled it from the cabinet and I saw her there, reading her astrology booklet at the table. I let the plate go and watched it shatter, a flower blooming in fast-forward, until all the pieces settled on the floor around my feet. My mamá didn't flinch.

"Mamá!" I screamed. "You don't even like Beto! What kind of father do you think he would be?"

Beto didn't want children, but still I thought he would be a good father. That wasn't the point, though. I just wanted her to talk to me, to argue with me, something.

She started rubbing small circles into her temples. She closed her eyes. I pulled four more dishes from the cabinet, all at once, and let them drop. One shard caught the side of my foot and sent a hairline of blood trickling down. She didn't look up until I grabbed a blue teacup—how could she have known that's the one I picked?—and was about to smash it, too. She opened her eyes, folded her hands in her lap, and said, "Your father gave me that cup." I felt my fingers tighten around the porcelain. She looked straight at me without blinking.

"He wasn't a good father," she said. "I always knew he wouldn't be. But everything he's given me, I've kept."

15.

In the depth of the night the giant rocks along Avenida Balboa seem to stand guard over our city. My mamá told me once there used to be a section of land that extended out over the bay where she and Papi would park. It's hard to imagine them like that, based on the people I know now, but when she told me about it I could see her face glowing with the embers of nostalgia and joy.

I climb over the rails and stand on a rock, the whole city behind me and the ocean and the rest of the world in front of me. I wonder what happened to that piece of land, and I think that even if the water swallowed it, there is still happiness that soaked into its dirt and even if my mamá or I can't stand on it now or touch it, it's still somewhere. Sometimes I think that's true: that every emotion gets caught in the fabric of the earth and even if it moves away from you and you can't find it anymore, it will always exist.

After another hour or so, I'm finally growing tired. On the way back to my house, I take a turn and walk to the church where I saw my papi nights before, expecting him to be on the bench again, gnawing at his seeds. I creep over the grass, looking for him. I don't know why. It's not like I'd have anything to say even if I found him. But he's nowhere around. And I start wondering if I really saw him at all the last time or whether he was just something I wanted to see. I feel a little crazy thinking things like that but it's just a night haze.

And then again, maybe people and things are the same as emotions: Even when you can't see them or feel them or be with them, and even when they have died and even before they are born, they still exist somewhere. Far away or close, they're always somewhere. Maybe nothing in the world is ever truly lost, I think. And then I snort a soft laugh. If Beto knew I was thinking stuff like that he'd say, "No, Marisol, some things *are* lost. Like your brain, you know."

16.

A few weeks later when I go to Beto's, Yasmine and Josefina are totally nude and I want to knock them out for having such perfect plastic bodies. This is how I feel these days. For a week I haven't been eating anything except soda crackers because pretty soon, I think, my empty stomach's going to set it loose, the thing inside me.

In his apartment, Beto says he might have found me a job.

"Is it legal?" I ask.

He looks wounded. I know the look—just a flash across his face. But he would never admit it.

"Forget it," he says.

I know I should apologize and ask him what the job is. My mamá and I are going to run out of money in a few more weeks and I don't want her to have to find work. But I stay quiet. Beto says it seems like I'm in a bad mood. I go over and finger his baby plant, which is drooping over the side of its pot.

"*Tu eres mi vida*, Marisol," he says, so sweetly. I love when he tells me that, that I'm his life, and I know he's trying to soften the harshness of a few seconds ago. He's always the one to come to me first. He wants me to smile but, instead, I start tearing up at the sound of it.

"Do you want to tell me something?" he asks. He's wearing a Pepsi T-shirt and cargo shorts and his old brown *chancletas* on his feet.

"No." I walk past him into the bathroom. I sit on the toilet for a while, waiting to see if anything happens but nothing does.

When I come out I know he thinks I've been crying because he's all, No reason to be depressed and whatever. He pulls a log of bills from his pocket. "This will make you feel better," he says, holding it up proudly.

"You did all that today?"

"School's out, remember? No one's watching around the playgrounds anymore. Plus, I had some suckers today. I jacked up the price a little on them."

"What are we going to do with it?" I ask.

"I think," he says, grabbing me around the waist, "we should go out and cheer you the fuck up."

17.

At the club, Beto offers to buy me a drink.

"Yeah," I say, "the strongest you can think of."

"That's my girl," he says, grinning. "We're going to have a good night, Marisol."

I watch him fight his way through about eight hundred people before he gets to the bar. He orders and while he's waiting for our drinks, a long-legged woman wearing tons of jewelry comes and puts her hand on his back. He nods at her and they exchange a few words, but she leaves after a minute.

"Who was that?" I ask when he returns, handing me a drink.

"I got you whisky with ice," he shouts into my ear.

"Who was that girl?" I shout back.

He shrugs. "She wanted to know if I had any weed."

We go out onto the dance floor for a while and it feels good, moving with him like that, our bodies bouncing off and around each other like electrons in our own charged field. I have on a short skirt, an electric-blue halter top, and sandals that make me taller. Beto rests his hand on the top curve of my ass and he keeps nuzzling his face in my neck. I send him for as many drinks as I can get down, trying to flood myself with poison, trying to drown it. Little by little, my legs start feeling lighter, my whole body lighter. My head is rolling around like it's loose on my neck and whenever I try to focus my eyes on something, I just see it pulsing and bright in front of me. There's one point when I slump down on Beto, who is the only reason I don't fall over altogether, and he props me up and asks if I'm okay. I just give him a drunken smile and he nods like, okay, now we're having a good time.

We go on like this until about two in the morning, when I feel a wetness on my thighs. I push off Beto and look down at his khaki pants. There's a brown-red bloom above the knee.

"*Que pasó?*" he yells.

I turn and run to the bathroom. It seems like hours before I finally get there and push my way into a stall. Ribbons of toilet paper are strewn over the floor and some putrid stench has found its home in there. I lower myself onto the toilet and sit for a long time, long enough until I'm sure it's washed away, like a whole weeklong period all at once and when it stops I wipe my fingers along the inside of my thigh and hold them up under the fluorescent lights. I don't know what I think I'll see. It just looks like blood. That it looks so normal in a small way makes me relieved, but at the same moment something else knocks into my lungs and something balls up like dough in my stomach and I start to feel nausea stalking through my body. I sit still and concentrate on breathing long enough to let it pass.

After I clean myself up, I find Beto and tell him we have to go.

"What the fuck's wrong with you? You see what you did to me? You got your period or something?" He's pointing to his pants.

"We have to go," I say again and turn from him quick, focusing my eyes on the door on the other side of the club to keep myself from crying.

18.

In the car, we pay at the tollbooth and roll the windows down. The air smells sweet, like mangoes and garbage.

We're on the highway, going forty or so, and I watch out the window as the trees slip past. We have the road to ourselves and after a while I tell Beto to go faster.

I can feel him look at me through the dark. "Are you going to tell me what happened back there?"

"Just go faster," I say.

"Would that make you happy?" he asks. He takes one hand off the steering wheel and brushes his fingers against my wrist. "I only want to make you happy."

"Go as fast as you can," I say.

I want it to be like my dream. I want us to just take off from this world, to be careening silently over everything, to be carried by the veins of the wind. The car roars a little and Beto jerks it into fifth gear. My hair whips like a fire around my head and somewhere in all this the trees I've been staring at stop looking like trees—it's just a wash of black-green velvet—and instead I see it all: my papi buying me a popsicle dipped in milk when I am young; my mamá, weeping as she hangs the laundry out to dry, using the sheets to dab her eyes; the first time I meet Beto, while I am leaving a shoe store on Avenida Central; the banana leaves brushing the wall behind our house in a storm; my pale blue dress years ago for my *quince años*; the tiniest round shape of the baby that died in me. But then the same thought comes to me again: maybe nothing is ever really lost. Even if you can't find it, even if you can't hold it in your thin, tired arms, it's always somewhere. The wind rushes against me like the sound of waves and I think, When we stop, I will tell Beto. Until then, we just drive.

MERCURY

For the third time since she has been here, Maria presses her ear to her grandparents' bedroom door, struggling to hear anything she can, something that might signal it's okay to go in. She flattens her ear so hard against the plywood door that she swears she can hear termites gnawing through the stringy wood, if there is even such a thing as termites here.

Two days earlier, when Maria landed at Tocumen International Airport, her grandmother, alone, was there to pick her up. Beyond the tinted automatic doors that opened every so often like a gaping mouth to reveal the crowd of people on the other side, craning their necks, anxious to catch a glimpse of those they were waiting for, Maria saw her grandmother watching. She saw her grandmother's coppery hair, pulled back, a few pieces poking out like wires and, after the customs agents had fished through everything in her suitcase and she went through the automatic doors herself, Maria saw that her grandmother looked older than the last time: her skin paler, her posture poorer, the sacks under her eyes heavier. But mostly Maria noticed that her grandfather wasn't there. Before she had a chance to ask, Maria's grandmother said, "Your *abuelo* isn't feeling right. He's at home resting." But then she laughed and drew Maria to her, brushing her powdered cheek against Maria's own, making it seem like everything was fine. On the way home in the taxi, her grandmother flitted her hands and spoke in Spanish so fast Maria had trouble keeping up. But she heard her grandmother clearly—because she said it twice—when she warned Maria not to bother her grandfather right away. "He is a proud man," she explained. "*Orgulloso*. He doesn't want you to see him until he's feeling better. He'll call you when he's ready. You understand?" Maria nodded her head, wondering when that would be.

Is he ready yet? Maria wonders now, her whole self pressed against the door. She wants to hear him breathing or coughing at least, but since she arrived, there's been no sound. She considers knocking but feels scared, though she's not sure why, of what might happen if she does. Her grandmother calls her from the kitchen to come for lunch. Maria sighs and pulls away from the door.

She walks with bare feet down the hallway to the kitchen. The air, like a constant hot breath from someone's open mouth onto her skin, spreads and folds around her. It carries the smell of garlic from the soup her grandmother is preparing for lunch. When Maria gets to the kitchen, she sits at the table on a chair with a rusted metal frame and a padded plastic seat, the backs of her legs sticking to it. She can feel the thick morning sunlight plodding in through the window and can smell the scent of dirt and the rooster dung coming from the backyard.

Her grandmother, in a threadbare pink nightgown, stands with her back to Maria, stirring *sancocho*—the same kind of soup she makes every day. When she serves it, the table is already set with big spoons on napkins and water glasses turned upside down to keep out flies. In the soup she puts half a cob of brown corn, a chunk of *ñame*, and strands of chicken meat. Sometimes, just for flavor, she drops in a chicken foot, something Maria has always regarded with fascination and disgust. Her grandmother presses white rice into a cup and delicately turns it onto a plate, like a sand castle, and serves it alongside.

"*Hola*," Maria says.

Her grandmother turns. "You're here!" she exclaims, and claps. Maria notices again how her grandmother's body bends slightly when she stands. Her grandmother pulls a brown paper bag from the top of the refrigerator. Inside, Maria knows, are the fresh and doughy bread sticks her grandmother buys every morning from a neighbor—Señora Carmen—down the street, who makes them herself. When Maria was younger and came here with her parents, they took her along in the mornings. She learned from her mother, who used to do it herself as a girl, to take a clean sock from the clothesline because the bread was always too hot to hold with her bare hands. Once, because he wanted to impress her, Maria's father tried to hold the bread without the sock. But he started bouncing the roll back and forth between his hands, small squeaks escaping him, and dropped it. Maria's mother had laughed in front of Señora Carmen, who had looked woefully at the roll on the floor, but Maria thought her mother had also seemed angry.

Maria eats the bread stick slowly, thinking of her grandfather in his bed. She rehearses in her head what she will say when she finally sees him—*Hola, Abuelo. Como te sientes? Me excitan para verte*—and quickly recognizes her error, reminding herself to use only the second-person formal when she talks to him, not the second-person familiar. How are you feeling? I'm excited to see you. She checks herself again to make sure the verb tenses are correct.

"You want oransh joose?" her grandmother asks, holding up a glass pitcher, laughing at her English.

"No, thank you."

"I"—her grandmother makes a squeezing motion with her hands—"to it myself."

"You squeezed it yourself?"

Her grandmother grins and nods.

"Maybe later," Maria says.

"You want *piña?*"

Her grandmother lifts an overturned plastic bowl from a plate to reveal a perfect wheel of sliced pineapple awaiting her.

"Okay," Maria says.

"*Piña, piña, piña, piña!*" her grandmother sings as she brings the plate to the table. When she places it in front of Maria, she points and says, "Pine-app-hol, no?"

Maria smiles. "Pineapple. *Sí.*" She can tell, by the way her grandmother tries her best with English, that she's still not entirely sure whether Maria can understand Spanish. After all, the last time Maria was there, she had known a total of about five words in Spanish. But since then she's been studying it in school with Señora Graham, who insists on addressing her students in Spanish even in the hallways. Her friends thought Maria had an advantage, since her mother spoke Spanish.

A boy who sat behind her—his Spanish-class name was Taco—even hissed at her once that he bet she secretly knew Spanish and was only pretending she didn't. Maria had wanted to tell him, No, my mother never spoke Spanish when I was little because she wanted me to be American, but she stayed quiet. At some point, Maria knows, her mother realized she had made a mistake in not passing on her language to her daughter. As soon as the classes were available, her mother called the guidance counselor to make sure they were on Maria's schedule. Maria would have signed up, anyway. And now she was doing well.

Her grandmother goes back to the stove to check the *sancocho*. She ladles some broth and lets it slide into a small bowl on the counter. "So that your grandfather eats something," she says, almost to herself. After she has collected enough broth, she replaces the lid on the cast-iron pot and turns down the gas.

"What will you do today?" her grandmother asks.

Maria answers, in Spanish, that she doesn't know. It's August. If she were home, she would be sleeping, or calling a friend, or eating Cheetos in front of the television. But she ended up here for the remainder of her summer vacation, because it was her mother's idea and because she wanted to come. The only people she knows here, though, are her grandparents. She is used to coming here with her parents, who always take her shopping or to the beach or to the restaurants by the canal or to the fruit markets. She is not used to figuring out for herself what to do here all day.

When Maria was younger her grandfather went with them to the ocean. He used to have a house there, overlooking the water. The house was painted bright yellow, with a wavy red roof. There were so many windows that even when you were inside, it never felt like you were. It felt, the whole time, like you were sleeping and breathing and eating with the chickens and the dogs and the beetles and the cockroaches. And then there really *was* being in the open air: Hammocks hung all around the house, tied up at the posts that supported the overhang in the roof, and tied up between palm trees. Maria and her grandfather used to rest in them—when she was still very small, they shared one and, when she got older, they each had their own—and gaze at the sea. Black silk, he would say, on the nights when the moon was new. Liquid mercury, when the moon was waning or waxing. A layer of butter melting in a frying pan, when the moon was full. Descriptions Maria gathered from her mother. This is what he's saying, Maria. This is what he's saying. They never spoke directly. And to Maria it felt like standing on opposite ends of a rickety bridge with her mother in the middle, bravely holding everything together, reaching out her arms in either direction, coaxing them both to come, but neither Maria nor her grandfather could comprehend how to walk to the other side.

Maria's grandfather sold that house years ago, though, because her grandparents needed the money. After that, her grandfather started calling her Mar, short for Maria, but it also meant ocean, she knew. He was trying to hold on to her and those days in the hammocks, he was trying to hold on to the house, he was trying to hold on to the ocean, but those things were gone. They had slipped through his fingers like the warm salt water itself.

Maria's parents are getting divorced. It came on, like a sickness you just can't shake, earlier this summer. Of course, it was probably even earlier than that, but the first time Maria remembers knowing it for sure was at the beginning of this summer.

They drove from their house in New Jersey up to Boston. Maria hadn't yet found a summer job and her father, wanting to take advantage of this rare opening in his teenage daughter's life, planned a trip to Boston. He surprised Maria and her mother with the news at the dinner table. As soon as he made the announcement, Maria's mother, an attorney, said something about a case she was working on that couldn't be abandoned. "It can," her father said, simply, firmly, and then looked to Maria for any objections. There was supposed to be a party at Dan Cavallano's house that weekend, but Maria didn't bring it up. A party was not important to her father at that moment, she could tell, and she wasn't positive she was invited, anyway. When she didn't offer anything, her father, his eyes crinkling at the corners, smiled and said they were really going to love the hotel he had set them up in.

In the car, her father played all his Chicago and America tapes.

"Only bands with geographical names!" he had shouted happily as they pulled out of the driveway. Her mother sat with her silver cell phone folded on her lap, staring out the window. In the back seat, Maria took her shoes off and put on headphones.

At the first rest stop, her father went for TCBY. Maria went to the bathroom and then came back outside to flip through her CD binder. Her mother was leaning against the car, squinting into the sun. If the backdrop were something other than a parking lot, Maria thought at the time, her mother could have been in an advertisement. Her mother was beautiful that way. Creamy olive skin, thick, wavy dark hair that fell halfway down her back, eyes rimmed with eyelashes so full she never needed eyeliner or mascara. She had been gaining weight lately, or at least often commenting that she had, but she had been exercising, too—on a tread-mill she bought and put in the basement—so she was more fit than she had ever been. She poked Maria's father in the stomach sometimes and asked if he wanted her to show him how to use the treadmill. But he always looked embarrassed and refused.

"What's your father getting?" Maria's mother asked, opening the car door enough to fit her voice through.

"Probably cinnamon swirl if they have it."

Maria pulled a CD from the sleeve and snapped it into her Discman.

"What do you think of this?" her mother asked.

"What?"

"This trip."

Maria shrugged. "I've never been to Boston."

"That's right. And maybe you wouldn't have wanted to go until you were thirty. Who said you had to go now?"

"Pop did."

"That's right." Her mother sighed. "Maybe I wouldn't have wanted to go until I was fifty." She looked thoughtful.

"Okay."

"But he just made that decision. Out of nowhere."

"It was supposed to be a surprise."

"I know. But I hate it sometimes how he decides things for me, about my life, without even asking."

Like what else? Maria wanted to say.

"Your father is not very good with surprises, you know." Maria's mother tapped a fingernail against her tooth. "Actually, there are a great many things in this world he is not very good at. When you get married," her mother said, turning to Maria and looking very stern, "marry someone who is better at things. At least at surprises."

To Maria, it sounded like her mother was saying: Marry someone better than him. But Maria didn't understand why planning a trip for the family out of the clear blue sky was such a big deal. The rest of the way to Boston, it kept coming back to her, how her mother was talking like she was angry about something else, how she was trying to find reasons to be angry, and how, even though she had seen her mother annoyed before, she had never seen her mother act quite like that about her father, twisting around his intentions in order to make a point, like she would do with a case. That's when, Maria remembers now, she started to suspect.

Maria decides that today she will write a letter to her grandfather. She will write it in Spanish. He sent her a letter once, on her fifteenth birthday, graceful blue ink sprawled across onionskin paper. She read what she could and looked up the words she didn't know. The letter talked about how she had made the transition to being a woman and how proud her grandmother and he were of her. She feels like much more of a woman now than she did then. Sixteen, after all, is the age in the United States when you finally begin to feel grown-up.

Maria's grandfather used to be a writer—a newspaperman, mostly, but he wrote short stories, too. She's been told he wrote one for her once, about a grasshopper, but she still doesn't know enough Spanish to read it. Maria's grandfather hasn't written anything new for years, though. He got clouds in his eyes—this is how her mother described it—and ever since then he has refused even to pick up a pen. Editors and friends begged him. But he was stubborn. "I can't write without my eyes," he said. "They're more important than my pen."

The last time Maria was here, her grandfather walked with a cane, tapping it against the baseboards as he walked. He could still see light, and he had become very good at sensing different shades of it—distinguishing honey from amber, white from the palest gray. Better to see these, he joked, than to see a rainbow in the dark. But everyone still worried. She remembers her parents and grandmother huddled around the kitchen table at night, talking about her grandfather, how he put on a show, how the fact that he was not writing said the most.

She remembers hearing her father offer a sum of money to send her grandfather to the best hospital. The sum was hundreds of times Maria's allowance and to her, it seemed very generous. No one at the table responded when he said it, though, and her mother simply covered his hand on the table with hers. Maria heard her mother say to her father later that night that he did not yet understand how things were in her country.

Maria pulls a chain hanging from the ceiling to turn on the lightbulb in the large hall closet. Stacks of boxes and papers lean against one wall and in the center stands a small metal foldout table with a typewriter on top. It is a manual typewriter, the one Maria's grandfather used. She has seen the typewriter before, on previous visits to her grandparents' house, but she has never touched it. The black keys are just barely concave and the letters that have been stamped on the heads of each one are wearing away. Worn into my grandfather's fingertips, Maria thinks.

When Maria begins typing, the clacking of the keys is slow and methodical. She has to work hard to get all the letters to show up on the paper, going back and retyping certain ones to make sure they don't get lost, sliding the carriage over again and again. When she misspells a word, she imposes a row of x's on top, because it's easier than using Wite-Out.

Querida Abuelo, she starts. She tells him what she has

been doing while she's been here, which is not much, really, but all of it near him, around him, sometimes only feet from him without him knowing any of it. She tells him how she believes her parents will get divorced even though her parents think they have been cunning about keeping this from her. She tells him how nervous she was on the plane on the way here because all Americans are nervous to fly these days, and how she missed seeing him at the airport when she arrived.

It's not very organized, but Maria doesn't care. She might not even give it to him. Someone would have to read it out loud to him, anyway.

Maria's grandmother walks past with an armful of laundry. She is heading outside and around back to the cement washbasin to wash the clothes by hand. When Maria was small her mother and grandmother used to stand her up in the washbasin to give her a bath. Once, Maria found a huge shell at the beach and brought it back to her grandparents' house. It sat on the table by her bed for a few hours until something poked its head out. Maria ran to her grandmother, who took the shell to that same washbasin and scalded it under hot water. She scooped the living part out—something slimy and gray—and let the shell dry on the grass under the basin. All so Maria could keep it and take it home in her suitcase when they left.

"Listen," Maria's grandmother says when she sees her sitting in the closet, still in her pajamas. "You shouldn't waste the day in this dusty box," nodding her head toward the closet. "You've been in here all this time?"

"I'm writing," Maria tells her in Spanish.

"Yesterday all you did was read the books you brought with you. Don't think I didn't notice."

"They're for school."

"I know you're not in school right now. School for you doesn't start until September."

Maria is daunted by the idea of trying to explain summer reading to her grandmother in Spanish, so instead she says, "I need to practice my writing."

"Ah! Ta-ta-ta-ta-ta," her grandmother says, clicking her tongue. "You need to go outside. Your grandfather used to go out and absorb everything and everyone. We used to know so many people. But now," she lowers her voice, "now that he can't see anything, he's bitter, thinking about how much more he could have set his eyes on when he had the opportunity. You need to go out. Writing is one thing, but experiencing life is more important. You understand?"

Maria nods because she understands the main parts.

"Go out then," says her grandmother. "You can walk to the supermarket to do some shopping for me."

Maria goes to her room to get dressed. On her way, she pauses again outside her grandparents' bedroom door and spreads her hand out on the rough wood. She glances toward the front of the house to make sure that her grandmother will not hear and then drums lightly on the door with her fingers. There is no sound from inside. Maria breathes deeply and then opens the door, just a crack, just to see him. She won't bother him, she thinks. He lies still, his hands on his chest as it moves up and down. His eyes are closed.

"*Abuelo,*" Maria whispers. The word hangs in the air and she can imagine it floating toward him. She smiles and closes the door behind her, then continues down the hall.

In Boston, they went to a very expensive restaurant for dinner. Maria's father wanted to go to Cheers, but her mother said, "It's a tourist trap, Jack. I've spent too many years already feeling like a tourist in this country. I just want to go out for a nice dinner." She had said it harshly, Maria thought, and Maria felt bad for her father for being on the receiving end of her mother's sour mood. Her father, after talking it over with the concierge at their hotel, made reservations for eight o'clock at a restaurant near the Common and told them both to be ready.

Maria had her own adjoining room this trip, as she had on trips for the past few years. Her mother resisted this setup every time. "We're a family. We live in one house, we can stay in one room!" she would argue. And every time, her father came to Maria's defense and said that teenagers needed their own space, and Maria's mother would counter that that was nothing more than an American myth. Usually, her mother would pout when they checked in to the hotel and in the ride up the carpeted elevators, and down the sterile hallways as they walked to their rooms. Maria was used to her mother knocking on their shared door in the wall a few seconds after getting into the room and asking if she could come over. Then she would admire the details of Maria's room, even though they were identical to her own, and remind Maria where they were staying, even though it was only on the other side of the wall, in case Maria wanted to come over and visit at any time. During this, her father would put his clothes in drawers, hang his sports coat if her mother had insisted he bring one, lie on the bed with his feet crossed, and watch the local news in order to learn more about the place they were visiting.

But in Boston, none of this happened. When they

checked in, they were silent. And when they got to their rooms, they stayed there, separate. A few times, Maria considered opening the door and going to her parents' side, but she kept waiting, sure her mother would knock and go through her routine soon enough. When the door finally did open, it was her father. He plopped himself on the second bed in Maria's room and asked her to change to channel five. Maria asked where her mother was. Her father said, "Well, she's not on this planet, I'll tell you that," and Maria didn't know whether or not she was supposed to laugh.

Later that night, in her own room, getting ready for dinner, Maria tried to listen through the door. She couldn't hear a thing. The restaurant was better, because there was noise swaddling them as soon as they walked in. The air in the restaurant glowed red, from the red lights overhead and the red glass votives on the tables. When they were seated, Maria's father ordered a bottle of red wine.

"That seems to be the order of the day," he said.

Maria's mother was surveying the menu. "Which one?" she asked. "The cod?"

"Red," her father said.

Her mother wrinkled her brow. "Red snapper?"

Her father sighed. "No. I was just saying how everything's so red in here that red wine was the obvious choice."

"Funny," her mother said, arching her eyebrows.

"So, do you like it?" her father asked Maria, waving his hand around to show he meant the restaurant.

"It's cool."

"That's what the concierge told me. Very cool. Very classy. Very anti-Cheers." He winked at Maria.

Maria looked to her mother.

"I don't know why you can never understand me," her mother started, putting down her menu. "I didn't need to come somewhere cool and classy. It's not that Cheers is a sports bar. I don't care about that. I could have gone to a million sports bars if they were regular neighborhood sports bars. I just wanted to eat somewhere that people would go if they lived here, to see the real Boston culture."

"Cheers *is* Boston culture," her father said.

"You know what I mean!" her mother said, raising the menu and slapping it down on the table, the leather making a dull thud against the tablecloth.

Her father reached across and covered the menu with his hand to keep her mother from banging it again. "I remember very clearly that you said you wanted to go out somewhere *nice.* Now you're saying we could have gone to a sports bar. What, exactly, is your definition of nice?" Her father was smiling, but not really.

Her mother leaned into him and looked straight

into his eyes. Maria twisted the corner of her napkin in her lap. "I don't know, Jack," her mother said slowly. "But it doesn't, at the moment, include you."

Something tough and dense ballooned in Maria's throat. She had never seen her parents like this with each other. Not even close.

A waiter delivered the wine to the table. Maria's parents pulled apart.

"It looks wonderful," Maria's father said when the waiter showed him the label. The waiter poured two glasses. Maria excused herself to go to the bathroom before she had a chance to see whether her parents would make a toast, like they sometimes did, or whether they would start drinking silently, on opposite sides of the table.

Maria is in her room, sitting on the edge of her bed, leaning over to buckle her sandals, when she hears a crash. She leaves the sandals unfastened and they flop down the hallway as she walks quickly to her grand-parents' room.

"What happened?" she asks. Her grandmother is standing rigidly beside the bed, white opaque glass scattered around her feet, a few pieces clinging to her nylons, which she wears with her brown plastic sandals.

Her grandmother is staring a pale, wide-eyed stare at her husband, still lying on his back. He looks the same as he did a few minutes earlier when Maria peeked in: his hands crossed on his stomach, cupped like he is hiding a snail underneath, his chest rising and falling with deep breaths. He is still sleeping.

"Are you okay?" Maria asks.

Her grandmother looks up, as if startled to see her. "I needed to change this lightbulb. Your grandfather had asked for a softer light."

"We'll clean it up."

Her grandmother nods, but Maria can see she is shaken.

"It's okay," Maria says. "An accident."

"I know."

Maria can see her grandmother is trembling slightly.

"He won't be mad," Maria says.

"Have you gone for the groceries yet?" her grandmother asks. When Maria shakes her head, her grandmother says, "Go."

Maria hesitates.

"I'll be fine here," her grandmother assures her.

At the Supermarket Rey, Maria imagines her grandmother cleaning up the glass from the floor, picking the shards from her nylons. She imagines her grandmother walking with unsteady legs and shaky breaths, blinking her eyes quickly like she so often does when she is visibly agitated so that the world, Maria thinks, comes to her in pieces, like slides inserted one by one into a film projector. She sees her bending down and holding the broom handle where it meets the bristles and sweeping the glass and the dust and the lightbulb filament into the dustpan and throwing it all away. Maria is only about a quarter of the way down the list—she has collected some mangoes in a plastic produce bag and salami spicy with peppercorns from the deli, two cans of condensed milk, and a bag of pork rinds—but suddenly she stops and walks out of the store. She leaves the food behind her, on the bottom shelf at the end of an aisle, and pushes through the revolving door. Outside, the sun is like a flash from a camera. A row of older men and women, mesh bags at their feet, delicate wooden tables like TV trays in front of them, are lined along the supermarket sidewalk, selling lottery tickets. When Maria was younger, her mother bought her a ticket once and she won three dollars. Everyone in Panama plays the lottery, her mother explained. And they watched, along with the rest of the city, the television show dedicated to announcing the winning numbers. When Maria saw that she had won, she and her mother went to wait in a long line with other winners to collect their money. Now, Maria considers buying a ticket again. Maybe it will bring good luck. Maybe it will bring just what her grandparents need. But in the next second she decides it doesn't matter. She just wants to get home.

A blue car is parked in the gravel driveway when Maria returns to the house. A sticker on the back windshield says MEDICO. Maria's feet and ankles are dusty from walking on the dirt roads to the store and back, but she does not bother to take off her sandals first and wash her feet with the hose lying in a lazy coil out front—something her grandmother usually insists that she do. Instead, she walks straight to her grandparents' bedroom.

The doctor, a short man with gray hair and a gray mustache, in a white shirt with a white undershirt visible underneath, stands beside the bed. His black leather bag is slumped on the floor at the foot of the bed. Maria hears her grandmother saying, "Three doctors. One when he was born, a second with the blindness, and now you. Be gentle."

"It's no problem," the doctor says.

"*Abuela,*" Maria says softly.

Her grandmother looks up and forces a smile. "Doctor, my granddaughter."

The doctor, his hand on her grandfather's forehead, does not acknowledge her.

"I came back to make sure you were okay. What's wrong?"

"I don't know. Doctor, do we know yet?"

The doctor shakes his head.

"I had trouble waking him up," her grandmother explains. "And he didn't want to talk to me when I did, except to tell me to call a doctor." She takes Maria's elbow. "Let's wait in the kitchen," she says.

The examination does not take long. Maria's grandmother melts a hunk of cheddar cheese on bread for Maria while they wait.

"If you had gotten the groceries, you could have it with salami, too," she says, then laughs, though nervously. "You can go back to the store after the doctor leaves."

When the doctor walks into the kitchen, leather bag in hand, he joins them at the table. Maria's grandmother becomes silent. Outside, a bird pecks at the window, chirps, and then flies off again. The air is hot and muggy. The tube lightbulb above them hums a steady buzz.

Finally, the doctor sighs and says, "We don't really need to be here."

"What does that mean?" Maria's grandmother says, suddenly angry. "I *know* you believe in God, Doctor. Of course we don't need to be here. But we are, we're blessed to be here, and my husband is no exception. If you're going to start telling me about the darkness that awaits—"

"Señora," he says, and sighs again. "I'm sorry. I only meant that there's no need to be in this room for me to say this. We could have had this conversation anywhere and your husband wouldn't know the difference."

Maria's grandmother wrinkles her eyebrows.

"I'm sorry, I'm not explaining well. This is difficult to say, but actually I'm quite sure. Señora, your husband is deaf."

Maria feels a rush through her stomach, up into her throat and back down again, and she watches as her grandmother shakes her finger at the doctor. "No," she says. "He could hear me yesterday."

"I don't think he could."

"Were you here yesterday? You didn't see him."

"I think he knows when you come into the room. I think there are vibrations he can sense to know when you're talking. And I think when he talks, he says the same things every day, because he assumes you do, too. He assumes when he says, 'I'm ready for lunch' or 'I'm feeling fine' that it makes sense because he's been saying those things in more or less the same order for a while now. How long has he been lying in that bed?"

"Two months," Maria's grandmother says softly.

"And over time, has he started to seem more disoriented?"

"He gives answers to questions I didn't ask. But only sometimes."

"I don't know why he waited so long to have you call a doctor. He must have known."

Maria watches her grandmother rise from the table. She looks as though she might fall.

"Abuela?" Maria calls.

But her grandmother doesn't respond. She brushes her hand in the air at Maria and begins to walk slowly from the kitchen.

When her family returned to New Jersey, her mother started calling lawyers. Maria knows this because there were messages from two of them one day when she came home from school. Just returning your call, they both said. Her mother knew a lot of lawyers, so maybe they were simply friends of hers, but Maria played the messages a few times and decided they sounded too formal for that. She wondered whether her father knew about these calls. She deleted the messages before either of her parents came home.

Maria was having trouble understanding it, how this had happened from one day to the next. A few weeks earlier, things were how they had always been——her father trying too hard, her mother rolling her eyes at his antics; her mother spoiling Maria with trips to the mall, her father sighing at the credit card bills; her parents taking Maria to her favorite pizza restaurant on Sunday nights. And now, suddenly, they were getting divorced. Maria was sure of that.

When she told her friend Denise about it on the phone, Denise said, "They were pretending before. I know you said you didn't see it coming, but they did that on purpose, you know? Like to spare your feelings. When my parents got divorced they tried really hard to keep it a secret. They were normal to each other for a long time even though they weren't normal underneath. They just didn't want me and Davey to see it, you know? But then the pot boiled over. As they say."

"I don't know if it's the same thing," Maria said, even though it sounded like it could be.

"I'm just saying. People can go for a long time fooling everybody around them. But eventually it comes out. You know Rico, from our health class last year? The same thing happened with his parents."

Maria said, "But my parents were actually happy before."

"I know," Denise said. "I'm really sorry."

Maria started looking for clues, watching her parents closely, analyzing their words and gestures and unconscious expressions. When she came downstairs in the mornings, she felt relieved when they were already gone because it meant that at least for a few hours, she wouldn't have to hear news of a divorce. The weekends were worse, because she always anticipated them together, at the table, waiting for her, even though they never were. And the days when her mother worked from home were nerve-racking, too, because there was always the possibility of her mother asking Maria to join her for her lunch break so that they could talk.

But Maria's parents didn't say anything. The bitterness and exasperation seeped through the house like steam; it spread all over, making the air stifling, but they didn't say anything.

Then, with the end of the summer approaching, one night they asked her to come into the TV room. Maria's father muted the television when she walked in. Her mother picked up the remote control and turned the set off completely. Her father rolled his eyes.

They were silent until her father asked, "So, how's your summer going?"

"Okay." Maria studied her parents' faces carefully, readying herself.

"Newspaper job's not the greatest?"

Maria had been answering phones—starting subscriptions and canceling them—for their local newspaper since returning from Boston.

"It's okay."

"I used to have a job in newspapers. Delivering them. This was before the Internet, of course, but I had a green bike with a basket on the front *and* one on the back, and at four in the morning—"

"Jack," Maria's mother interrupted. "What are you talking about?"

"I already know what's going on," Maria blurted.

Her parents looked surprised.

"We bought you a plane ticket to Panama," her mother said. "Is that what you mean?"

"What?"

"We thought it would be nice for you to see your grandparents, to go away. You've been working hard all summer."

"You're not going?" Maria asked.

"It's a direct flight. Your grandparents will be at the airport to pick you up. You'll be fine." Her mother smiled worriedly, as if she was afraid Maria could see right through her to what was really going on. And even though she could, she also kind of wanted to go, to leave her own house for a while, to get a continent away.

"For how long?"

"A week," her mother said.

"What do you think?" her father asked.

"Give her a minute," her mother said.

"I'm not allowed to talk?" her father shot back.

Maria's mother stared at him blankly.

"I said, *talk*! Am I allowed to do that anymore or do I need written permission?"

Maria felt alarmed, watching them. It was like they

lacked the skills to communicate with each other anymore. It was as if, when her father spoke, her mother looked at him and saw a little goldfish, popping open his mouth over and over again but making no sound. And when her mother spoke, her father looked and saw a piranha doing the same thing.

"I'll go," Maria said finally, and everybody looked relieved.

Long after the doctor leaves, Maria gets up from her chair. The world around her has grown a sort of chocolate dark, the lights from the city keeping it from getting completely black. The moon is a sliver in the sky and she thinks, mercury. Tonight it must be mercury.

For hours, Maria has been imagining the conversations she and her grandfather could have had and now never will. She wanted to show off her Spanish. She wanted to have a conversation with him by herself for the first time.

Her grandmother went straight to the bedroom and hasn't come out since. Maria assumes both her grandparents are sleeping by now. She wonders if she should call her mother. Her parents gave her a phone card before she left so that she wouldn't add to her grandparents' bill. The card is on the table beside her bed, next to a pot of lip gloss. It seems like her mother should know. But Maria's mind turns again to her grandfather. We will never have a conversation, she repeats to herself. It's like being hollowed out inside, everything scraped away but sadness.

There are tears on her face when she begins, too, to think of her parents, who speak the same language but cannot understand each other.

Maria walks through the dark to her room. At the foot of her bed is the letter she wrote earlier that day. She tears it into quarters and pushes the pieces into the dust under her bed with her toe. Then she makes her way down the hall to her grandparents' room. She doesn't knock and she doesn't wait. She opens the door and crawls onto the bed between them, on the pilled sheets, and closes her eyes. Her grandmother breathes heavily with her head on her arm. The air smells of medicated cream and mothballs. Maria traces *Good night*, in Spanish, on her grandfather's forearm. She whispers, *"Buenas noches,"* to her grandmother in the dark. Then she goes to sleep and dreams of everything else she wants to say.

BEAUTIFUL

And then that summer when the heat felt like wading through molasses and the streets hummed in a desperate sadness all day and all night, God came down from heaven and paid a visit to our family in two ways: My father returned home and my uncle got rich. The second way happened first and there were many people later who would say that it was the only reason my father returned, that he must have heard the news about his brother and wanted to cash in, but at the time they were just two unrelated miracles as far as I was concerned. And I was thankful.

My Tío Arrocha calls my mamá first thing in the morning to tell her the news, to tell her he's won the lottery for real this time, the big prize, he's done it, and I can hear him hollering right through the phone. I am standing in the hallway watching as she runs to the television in her slippers and thin nightgown, the telephone against her ear. She picks up the green notebook that she keeps in the drawer and opens it and looks at the numbers she has written down, all in pencil, in rows and rows, like an army marching on the page, and traces along with her finger. She starts nodding, Yes yes, wait, what was the last one? Yes, oh, JesusMaryandJoseph, you really did it! and crosses herself over and over and stands up and sits down and stands up again, walking around in circles.

The front door is open like it always is except when we're sleeping, and through it, through the coconut trees at the edge of our property, I can see two dogs that our neighbors keep in their yard behind a fence. I smile at the dogs from inside the house.

Mamá gets off the phone after a good while and I run back into my bedroom, sliding on the tile floor in my socks, and quick lie down in my bed. She comes in smiling, flushed, looking like she's ready to burst, like my friend Charito when she tries to hold her breath underwater for too long. Mamá tells me to get up because Tío Arrocha is on his way over.

What for? I ask, because I want her to tell me what's going on with the lottery and everything; I want to

know how much money he has now——my rich uncle!——
and I am pretending like I don't know anything about it
yet. But all she says is, Tío Arrocha is coming over to
take you out. I look at her once more with pleading in
my face, but she's hardly even there. Her face is a pink
balloon all filled up and she's floating out of the room,
bouncing around against the air.

When my uncle comes over I am waiting on one of the
plastic-covered chairs that are like sitting on taffy. I am
wearing my best clothes, which means a pair of brown
sandals, even though one of the buckles is broken so I use
a safety pin to keep it together; a pale lavender dress that
was pilled in the skirt so Mamá stitched a white apron
onto the front to fancy it up; and a headband to hold
back my hair, which I spent all last summer growing out
and that Mamá says looks best when it's pulled back off
my face. Because I have such a pretty face, she explains.
Mamá's smoothing down my hair when Tío Arrocha
comes in and she shrieks and runs to him and gives him
one glorious hug. He's laughing and telling her it's not
like he did anything, just got lucky is all. But Mamá is
glowing like Jesus Christ himself walked into our house.

Tío Arrocha looks at me and says, I was thinking,
Rosaria, that you deserve a brand-new dress. I sit up

straighter at the sound of this and he says, I know a place in the city. He extends his hand to me and I'm up on my feet ready to go. He's always been my favorite uncle even though he lives way over in a poor part of town where all the walls of the houses are splitting wood and all the roofs are sagging. But he's a good man, my mamá always says, one of the best men I know. Not all of them are like that.

We take a banana-yellow taxi to the store. The banana-yellows are the nicer ones but they cost more money. When Mamá and I have to take a cab we take the black ones with the ripped seats and the windows that are stuck so they never roll down and the drivers who are new so they almost never know any of the shortcuts that even Charito and me know just from playing around town. On the way to the store I see the same people on the streets as always: the man who peels fruit with a plastic razor and hands the skins to birds; the kids who are building a fort out of shopping carts tipped up on their sides; the men playing dominoes, always wearing their *guayaberas* and their nice hats like they're playing dominoes with the president. Then we start passing nicer places—jewelry stores with names like Mercurio and Reprosa, and skyscrapers made out of glass. It feels far away from Avenida Central, where my mamá usually takes me to shop.

In the dress store we walk up to the counter and my

Tío Arrocha talks to the mustached man who's working there and tells him to let me try on anything in the store. The man looks at me and smiles. He says he doesn't know if there is anything in the store pretty enough for a girl as pretty as me. Then he bends down and winks and tells me he'll be right there at the counter when I find something I like.

Tío Arrocha takes me by the hand. We look at the racks along the wall and at the dresses that hang from the ceiling, falling around us like the downpours that come for a few minutes at a time during the rainy season when all you can see are the big bloated water drops coating the whole world. I almost stop breathing because the dresses are so perfect. More perfect even than my first communion dress, and more perfect than Charito's mom's wedding dress, which we play in sometimes since her mom says she doesn't care a thing about that dress anymore ever since Charito's dad left.

The dress we end up taking has a white top with a little bow, big, round, white, puffed-out sleeves, white ruffled trim along the bottom, and a red satin skirt that spreads out like the fans the ladies use in church. Tío Arrocha says I am the most beautiful girl he has ever seen. The mustached man behind the counter agrees, so it is settled. We pay, and the mustached man wraps it up and even though I walk out in my old lavender dress, something about me feels new.

The banana-yellow taxi drops us off at home and when we walk inside Papá is standing there. Just like that. Even though I haven't seen him in a few years, I recognize him right off because of old photographs and, I suppose, just because I remember. Tío Arrocha stands still at first but then walks over to him, shakes his hand, gives his brother a pat on the back, and mumbles a few things that I don't hear. My mamá runs out from the kitchen, wiping her hands on a towel, looking a little red in the face, and says quietly, Jorge's come back to us. The way she uses his first name makes me think she is talking more to Tío Arrocha than to me. But that's all she says. I am near the door with my new dress hanging over my arms, the plastic wrap sticking to me.

We should go out and celebrate, she says next. All of us. I think that would be nice. She looks around again and you can see the pleading in her eyes like she is helpless, like a cotton ball in a tornado. Rosa, you could wear your new dress, she says. We are standing in the silence, lodged in it like fossils, the minutes stretching out patiently around us until, finally, a snap.

Yes, I think that would be fine, Tío Arrocha says. We'll go tomorrow night. I'll come by the house tomorrow night at six-thirty.

My mamá looks pleased, beams at him, and tells

him we will be ready at six-thirty sharp and so, until then. Tío Arrocha nods to Papá once more and walks out, stopping to kiss me on the head, just barely on the top of my hair, before leaving.

Mamá tells me to come and give my papá a hug, which is what I have been dying to do. I put my dress down carefully and run to him. I wrap my arms around his waist and press my face into his belly, against his white cotton shirt that smells like gasoline jumbled with soap. I breathe him in and hold on. He bends down and gives me a hug good and proper and tells me oh, he's missed me so much. How old are you now? he asks and I tell him eight. And he mumbles that he can't believe how much I've grown. After a minute Mamá says, Okay you two, now everything's back to normal, so good. And then she suggests that I go try on my dress for them.

I leave my old sandals in the bedroom and am barefoot when I come back out. Papá makes a fuss. You've gotten so pretty since the last time I saw you, look how much your hair has grown—all the way down your back, are you making good grades in school, you look like a princess in that dress, how long it's been! I am a caterpillar and a butterfly at the same time—unsure of the attention, wanting to stay hidden, but also feeling like I've broken into a new life where I am more glittering and confident and have left the other one behind. I practice curtsying and spinning and I laugh with Papá until I can hear the yucca frying and I can smell the garlic from the *sancocho* filling up the air and Mamá finally tells me to go change for dinner and to wash please before I come to the table.

That night I have two parents to kiss me good night. Falling asleep I think about how lucky I am for that. Charito and I are forever wishing for our papás to come back even though Charito's mom says we are all better off with them gone. But she never knew my papá and she wouldn't say that if she knew. Before he left, he used to play with me, take me on walks, and swing me around in the air like a carousel. He would take me to the swimming pool at the Intercontinental Miramar Hotel, sneak me in like we were guests, and we would splash around doing belly flops. I try to remember, as I fall asleep, why Mamá told me he left but I'm not sure I ever knew.

I wake up later to my door creaking open. Papá is standing in my room. I think maybe he is confused because he hasn't been here in so long he can't remember which room is his. So I whisper, Papá, this is my room, but he doesn't move. I can't even tell if his eyes are open or not. It's almost like he's a ghost, swimming through the dark. Maybe he's walking in his sleep like the people on the streets at night, so I start to get up to help him back to his room but he whispers, No, stay where you are, it's okay. And there is something about how he says it's okay, because I hadn't even asked, that makes me feel like it's not. A few seconds later he starts in a little zigzag over to my bed and I think maybe he just wants to talk because he's missed me so much. But then he gets into my bed, under the covers, like I do sometimes with Mamá when the rain is too hard and the thunder too loud. I can feel him. I can feel the warmth of him, his woolly cheek against my face. I can hear him breathing deep and low. I can smell him, still like gasoline and soap but also sweet and watery like alcohol when he breathes out. I am lying rigid, a plank of wood, a tree that's fallen over into my bed. He is playing with my hair, winding it around through his fingers, and he tells me I have hair like silk, hair like a waterfall, hair like a million rivers. I am still confused about why he's here in my bed and when he talks the words all fall over on top of each other, like a row of dominoes. He kisses my forehead and the tip of my nose and his mouth trips down to meet my mouth. But it's not the same kind of kiss he gave me when he first saw me. It's harder and longer like the people I see on the television, like I saw Mamá kiss Tío Arrocha once when they thought I wasn't looking, full on the mouth.

And suddenly I am more than just confused, I am scared, trembling like a little baby. I try to draw my head back deep into the pillow but he moves with me. I try to wiggle away and twist my head, to drag my lips away from his, but he is holding on to my hair with one hand and pulling it until I feel it breaking from my scalp, pulling it like he thinks he owns it and is trying to take it for himself. So I stay put and try to force up a sound from my throat but it gets stuck there. All around my mouth it is wet and his other hand, the hand that's not in my hair, is against my belly now, under my nightshirt, and I try to slide out from under him. I dig my heels into the bed but he is pulling my hair harder now and still kissing and moving his hand around in a circle on my belly, his fingertips passing just under-neath the elastic band of my pajama shorts, his nails scraping along my skin, his sour breath unfolding against my cheek again and again. I would give up everything, I would give up my brand-new dress, to make this stop, I am thinking, when all of a sudden it does. It stops. His hand falls away onto the mattress between us and his fingers loosen in my hair. When I look over, he is sleeping beside me.

I am breathing hard. My eyes are wet. My mouth is wet. I stare up at the ceiling, trying to figure out what just happened, trying to remind myself that my papá is a good man, trying to tell myself that he didn't mean any of it. I want to get up, I want to get away from him and figure all this out; I want to get away from the smell of his alcohol breath, which is low and regular now that he's sleeping. But I can't move at first, scared because I don't want to wake him. Finally, after what feels like a whole year, as quietly as I can, I get out of the bed, scoot down to the end, and creep off. I turn around and look at him. Something swells inside me, something hateful and thick and hurtful and sad, and at that moment more than anything else in the world I want to get as far away from him as I can. I want to sink to the middle of the earth, I want to float out to the middle of the ocean. The back of my head is burning, throbbing, like his fingers are still there in my hair, holding me down. It's like fire spreading out and I reach up to try to stop it but I don't even want to touch my hair anymore, I don't want to put my fingers through the pieces like he did. I feel sick at the thought of it touching my back now, hanging off my head, ready to be pulled again. And before I know it, I am standing, with the door locked, in the bathroom, up on the wooden step stool, looking in the small, wavy mirror. I am cutting it all off, as close to the roots as I can get and promising myself that he will never never never again be able to hold me like that. I cut the millions of rivers of hair until it's all dried up and washed out and can be filled with nothing but wind. Little by little, I feel the fire cool.

In the morning I am gone. I spend half the day at the old rotten beach by the construction zone and in the afternoon I go over to Charito's. She laughs when she sees me. Look at your hair, she says. What did you do? I tell her I cut it but I don't tell her why. She shrugs and says I am crazy and that now I will have to be the boy whenever we play for sure, then giggles again and shakes her head. We spend the afternoon playing and when we dress up I can't believe my eyes when I see myself in the mirror again, the first time since last night, my hair sticking out all over the place like a pineapple top. I stand there looking at what I've done. There is something about it that I like. It feels like a wall that he won't ever be able to get through again and like maybe I am not even the same person he touched in the first place.

My mamá calls late in the day to see if I am over at Charito's and to remind me about the dinner tonight and to come home soon and get cleaned up and to wear my new dress and be ready for Tío Arrocha to pick us up. This morning I had forgotten all about the dress. I didn't even tell Charito about it—the beautiful dress that will make me the perfect new me. Charito's mom yells up to us and tells me to hurry, I don't want to be late, my mamá made it sound like a very important dinner. As I walk downstairs on my way out she stops me and asks what in the devil I did to my hair. Did Charito do this to you? she asks. I did it, I tell her. And when I say it, I feel proud. I hope you didn't just do it here, she says, because your mamá is going to hit the ceiling when she sees this and I don't want her calling me about it. Then she laughs and runs a hand over the patchy pieces and says, Actually, I sort of like it, Rosa. Then she tells me to go on home.

I walk to my house, past the lottery vendors and a man selling popsicles and condensed milk, and when I arrive the only thing I want to do is go straight to my room and put on my dress and feel beautiful perfect wonderful and stay inside the wall I built that he can't get past.

My dress is hanging in plastic on the back of the closet door. I take it down and put it on along with my old best sandals, although even they look different now—you hardly notice the safety pin anymore—and I practice my curtsys, spreading the skirt out and letting it fall again and again and again until finally I hear my mamá calling me to come out please. Tío Arrocha will be here any minute and we want to see you, Rosa, we want to see our little girl. I feel like God is reaching down his giant hand and scooping me up, holding me, carrying me, when I walk out to where both my mamá and my papá are waiting. My mamá turns around and drops her purse and throws her hands over her mouth and says, What have you done to yourself? Is this a joke? Oh, Rosa! What a cruel joke to play on me and on your papá, especially, who hasn't seen you in so long and now, to see you this way! Did Charito do this to you? She gets louder and louder. Papá says quietly, Who did this to you? And I know he knows the answer to his own question. We both know it was him, really. But he doesn't say anything else, just stands there in black pants and a gray *guayabera*, his cheeks a little flushed, as Mamá goes on in a voice that rattles, You must have the devil in your soul to do something like this! On today of all days! Tío Arrocha will be here any minute. We can't go out to dinner with you looking like this. She starts pacing around and looks up and shakes her hands and holds them out like she is waiting for an answer to fall down from heaven to explain. You've ruined every-thing, Rosaria. You were going to look so pretty in your dress and Tío Arrocha was so kind to buy it for you and now look what you've done!

I stare at Mamá and wonder if she knows what really happened, what my papá is really like, and because I know the truth, I think how crazy she sounds. She goes on and on and still Papá says nothing. But she could go on and on forever and even if Papá said some-thing, I wouldn't be listening. I just stand there feeling more beautiful than ever.

CHASING BIRDS

Maybe it had been raining for years. By the second night, it was easy to feel that way. They had come to this spot, in the heart of Panama, two days ago and even then it had been raining. There was no sign of respite. It was as if they had come to a different universe, where threads of rain were laced through the air, as if rain were just part of the atmosphere, something that had always been there and always would be, as if rain here was simply a fact. The corrugated zinc roof that stretched over their room acted like a giant drum, exaggerating each ping of dropping rain until it sounded like pebbles were crashing from the sky.

A ruffle of thunder unfolded. June closed her eyes.

She hoped the roof wouldn't cave in. Then she remembered that earlier that day she had leaned her whole weight against a window and it hadn't shattered the way she thought it might. So maybe the roof would hold after all.

"Harv," June whispered. The room smelled like old wet washcloths. "Harv." She waited as another surge of thunder reeled across the sky. "Harvey," she said, loud enough to be heard. He didn't move. "Harvey!" she shouted, but the pounding symphony on the roof drowned her out. "I want to leave!" she screamed.

The city had leapt up and taken June by surprise. She was expecting something smaller, more rural. But after they rented the car and started driving, she saw a huge, bustling capital, poor but inescapably vibrant. She peered out the tinted windows of their small car, her purse tight between her knees, as Harvey drove and fiddled with the air-conditioning. There were more billboards than she had seen anywhere, clumped along the side of the road, many of them blank, many of them peeling. Banks and hotels and apartment high-rises rose up around them, everything built into hills of untended, tall, wispy grass freckled with tiny flowers.

They didn't get lost, not once. Something Harvey was extremely proud of. When they pulled off Avenida Balboa and into the roundabout in front of the Intercontinental Miramar Hotel, it was clear they had come into a wealthy pocket of the city. The glass buildings were triumphant and imposing, and the giant, delicate arms of construction cranes swayed over them.

Harvey handed the car over to the valet. "Where will you park it?" he wanted to know.

The valet pointed to a lot at the side of the hotel, the front lip of which dropped straight down into the bay.

"Make sure it doesn't fall in there. This is a rental," Harvey said.

The valet nodded.

"It's not my car," Harvey said, as if he were talking to someone hard of hearing.

The valet nodded again. It was hard to tell whether he understood.

The next morning, while they ate fried corn cakes and ham at Restaurante Boulevard, the waiter told them that the very thing Harvey was afraid of had happened just last week. The valet hadn't used the parking brake and the car had rolled right off the edge, plunging into the water. The waiter laughed. "The car try to escape. It want to swim," he said, and Harvey and June just nodded.

. . .

They were in the city only one night but it was enough time to feel overwhelmed. Appleton, Wisconsin, where they lived, where June had spent her whole life, suddenly seemed so tidy and manageable in comparison. Here, the city felt boundless around her. As if she were no more than a small crumb in the center of it, and it ebbed in concentric circles around her and around her, endlessly outward. It seemed so easy to lose the sense of your own place in a city like this, to lose the sense of your place in the world entirely.

But then, they were out. After checking on the car from their window at least fifteen times during the night, Harvey retrieved it and drove them away. They had come to chase birds, after all. One night in the city was for June, who had said before they left that she wanted it. She wanted to see something in Panama besides birds. And she had wanted the possibility of romance—staying in a hotel in a foreign country with her husband. But Harvey had drunk too much wine with dinner and fell asleep as soon as they returned to their room. There was still time, June reasoned. They were switching hotels but there would still be the romance of a foreign country.

The air conditioner in the car blasted stale, humid air. June reknotted the scarf in her hair. She had applied lipstick this morning, something she never did. It was a shade of coral and she had purposely kissed Harvey on the cheek and then tried to be coy, saying, Oops, I left a mark, and smudging it clean with her thumb. Harvey had seemed annoyed, rubbed his skin with the heel of his palm, and then went to the checkout desk. As they pulled away from the city limits, June stared at razed red hills; the land in the rain turned to the color of rust. Palm trees hovered over them as they bumped along roads missing chunks of pavement.

When they arrived in Gamboa it was still raining, long dashes of water impelled from the sky.

"This is it," Harvey announced, stopping the car on a gravel pass, the tires crunching as if they were chewing the ground beneath them.

June craned her neck and looked up through the car window.

They would be staying in what used to be a radar tower occupied by the U.S. Air Force but had been transformed into a hotel, the rooms flush with the soaring canopy of trees in the rain forest surrounding them.

"What if there's lightning?" she asked.

"Then there's lightning." Harvey peered in the mirror and smoothed the hairs of his beard with his fingertips.

"Do you really think it's safe?"

He didn't answer.

"Harvey."

"Safe? No. But that's the point. It's a risk, it's an adventure. That's why we're here."

He squeezed her arm.

"Oh," she said.

"Come on," Harvey prodded, and before June knew it, he was out of the car.

This was their first trip together outside of the United States, not including the time they went to the Canadian side of Niagara Falls during their honeymoon three years ago. When she was young, June had vacationed with her parents in places like Charleston, Napa Valley, and Annapolis. Over the past three years, camping had become June and Harvey's primary lure—June bathing in glassy lakes and drying herself on warm rocks while Harvey hiked and chased birds. She used to ask him to join her, describing how they could paddle out through the water, their chins skimming the surface. He told her simply that he preferred the air to the water, but in time she learned that he said it only because he didn't know how to swim, one of the few vulnerabilities he would admit.

Bird-watching in Panama was something Harvey had learned about in an e-mail from American Airlines.

The e-mail claimed that Panama was home to over nine hundred fifty species of birds. It said that Canopy Tower in Gamboa, near the canal, was the best place to see them. They bought new luggage and ordered passports and listened to a set of tapes that June had checked out from their local library with the aim of learning Spanish. Now, the only phrase she could remember was "Let's go to the discotheque." *Vamos a la discoteca*. She had been so excited about traveling, though. Excited about a getaway with Harvey. In the beginning, she had thought camping would be that: Harvey and she under crisp black skies dotted with stars, cuddling together in sleeping bags. But it was always more practical than that, less tender. This trip to Panama would be different, she was sure.

The room was small and clean. It was shaped like a piece of pie with the tip cut off. Two twin beds were pushed against the outer walls, following the angle inward until the bottom corners of their mattresses almost touched. A ceiling fan hung overhead and nearly the entire curved wall behind the heads of the beds was made of glass, so that from their perch in the tower the treetops came up to their feet, a luxurious green carpet that stretched for miles.

"It's like a tree house," Harvey said, dropping his suitcase on one of the beds. He was giddy.

The day was bright despite the rain. June nodded and sat on the opposite bed. Drops of water ran from her wet hair down her neck. Harvey had already located his binoculars. June had bought them for him two Christmases ago, but now she wished she hadn't. She was surprised at how annoyed she suddenly felt. She watched him draw the lenses within a hairbreadth of the glass wall, and then slowly move his head up and then down.

"Don't get too close," she said.

"To what?"

"The glass. I don't want you to push through."

He didn't say anything.

She sighed and ran her palm over the stiff bedspread. "This is a nice place," she said. "I'm glad we came." She was trying.

Harvey lowered the binoculars and turned around. His sunglasses dangled around his neck from a yellow foam strap. "See? It will be fun."

"The room is nice."

"It has a great view."

"Did you ask for a room with a queen bed?"

"I didn't specify." He had turned from her again. "There are supposed to be hundreds of tanagers and flycatchers out here. If we're lucky, we might even see a rufous-breasted ground-cuckoo."

The next day, Harvey went out in the rain with the guide, Raul Sanchez de Arenas. Harvey put on a bright orange poncho and stuffed tissues into his shorts pockets to wipe the binocular lenses when they got soaked, but when June suggested he ask Raul about getting some galoshes, he refused and insisted on wearing his loafers. June promised Harvey that she would go out with him tomorrow. The rain would have to let up by then, she said, even though, as she said it, she knew it probably wouldn't.

June was pleased to find a library in the lobby, or something that passed for a library in the room that passed for a lobby. She stood in front of the bookcases and ran her fingers lightly over the spines of the oversized volumes. They were mostly ecological guides. A few novels lined the bottom shelves, but they were all in Spanish so she replaced them one by one. Finally, June selected a book with color photographs of moths.

She had the lobby to herself. She stretched open a hammock strung between two poles, pulling its sides out like an accordion, and settled into it cautiously, afraid that it wouldn't hold, afraid that it would pull the posts down and the entire tower with it. Eventually she relaxed and opened the book, resting it on her stomach.

A few minutes later, she heard footsteps. She sat up as quickly as she could, the hammock swinging away beneath her and rolling her off. She clutched the book to her chest.

A hotel employee smiled at her and nodded.

She nodded back.

He leaned sideways and peeked at something on the desk, fanning one paper aside to look at the one underneath. Then he walked toward her.

"You read?" he asked, in English.

"Yes."

"It is good?"

June moved her arm from where she was still clutching the book to show him the cover.

"Moths," she said.

He appeared only slightly younger than she, thin filaments of silver running through his dark hair. He wore khakis paired with a green polo shirt, the hotel's logo embroidered on the chest. And he smelled like talcum powder, like something utterly dry in the midst of all this rain.

"*Polillas*," he said.

He stared at her and she realized he was waiting for her to repeat it, that he was trying to teach her something.

"*Polillas*," she said.

He smiled again. He didn't show his teeth when he smiled, but his eyes crinkled at the corners.

Then, "I see you at dinner," he said, and walked past her.

June turned to watch him. Where was he going? Where was there to go? She sighed and returned the book to its spot on the shelf. She wandered to the window to look out. She remembered telling Harvey yesterday not to push on the glass in their room. Out of nowhere, she had the urge to do it. She spread the fingers of her right hand like a web and touched her fingertips to the glass pane. She pushed gently. Then a little harder. Nothing happened. She flattened both palms against the window and leaned her whole weight on her hands, her thin body at an angle, her arms bent until her chest was brushing the glass. When finally she stood up straight again, she felt shaky, not herself, as if she had just walked a tightrope or dashed across a busy street.

By the time Harvey returned, June was napping on her bed. Harvey woke her when he walked in and stood over her, drops of water sliding off the tips of his poncho and onto her elbow. She had fallen asleep with a butterscotch candy in her mouth and when she opened her eyes, she felt it, stuck to the inside of her cheek. She worked it loose with her tongue and sat up.

"Hi," Harvey said, grinning.

The inside of her mouth felt thready, like a shag carpet.

"How was it?" June asked. She felt happy to see him.

Harvey began peeling clothes from his body.

"It was incredible. If I started to tell you about all the birds we saw, I would be talking until tomorrow." Harvey propped open his suitcase lid. He rummaged through dry clothes.

June rubbed her eyes and noted, with vague despair, the sorts of things Harvey had packed: sneakers, boots, a Windbreaker, a multi-pocket vest, field guides, film canisters, binoculars, and extra lens caps. She had packed perfume and lipstick and a new nightgown. "Did you make notes?" she asked. "In your journal?"

"Of course. Of course I did. But I think you had to be there. It was absolutely incredible."

Harvey was sitting on the edge of his bed now, shirtless, pulling off his sopping socks. He propped up one foot at a time on his knee. June stared at the bottoms of his feet. They were wrinkled like the rippled surface of a lake.

"What have you been doing?" he asked.

"Nothing."

"Anything good in those magazines?" He pointed to a short stack of cooking magazines June had brought with her, on the floor next to her bed. She was a chef by trade, though she had worked in a restaurant only briefly and, since then, had taught cooking classes at a community center in Appleton and at private parties. That's how they had met: Harvey was attending a class under June's tutelage. Typically when men enrolled in her class, they did so to impress a woman and Harvey was no exception. Because of his age—early fifties, she guessed—June had assumed he was there to learn to make something for his wife. He told her after the first class, though, that he'd been divorced for years—back in the sea, he'd said—though he'd been hooked recently by a French professor at the junior college where he, too, taught. When he said, "You see? It's like that saying 'Lots of fish in the sea.' That's what I was referring to," June let out a snort of laughter and then hid her face. "Right," she said, when she had composed herself. But still, she found him attractive, and she was lonely, so when he showed up in her class three weeks later to announce that he'd been released by the French professor back into the sea and to ask if June would like to go out to dinner, she said yes.

"I learned how to say 'moth' in Spanish," she said.

Harvey pulled off his wet boxers and sat naked on the bed.

"What is it?"

"*Polilla.*"

"I think maybe I knew that."

"No you didn't."

"How do you know whether I did or not?"

She sighed.

Harvey shrugged. "Time for a shower. Dinner's at eight tonight."

"I think maybe I knew that," June said.

"Funny girl!" Harvey shouted at the ceiling, and walked into the tiny bathroom at the tip of their pie-shaped room.

When they got to the dining room and sat down, June felt herself looking for the hotel employee. There was something comforting about knowing someone else in this strange country, even if she hardly knew him at all.

Among the maybe ten people at the table, he sat diagonal from her. The hotel was run like a bed-and-breakfast; everyone, even the staff, ate together. During dinner, while Harvey was preoccupied talking to a guest from Germany, the employee asked her name.

"Shoon," he said, after she told him.

"June."

"Choon."

"June."

He nodded.

June hoped she hadn't embarrassed him, but he didn't say anything else to her after that.

Later, when everyone had finished, June waited for Harvey in the hallway leading from the dining room. She would have gone to the room herself, but she realized on the way there that only Harvey had a key. She was considering going back to ask him for it when the hotel employee passed her in the hallway. He stopped when he saw her.

"You are okay?" he asked.

June nodded. The hallway was a hazy amber color from the dim floor lamps. She could hear Harvey talking from where she stood.

"It is your husband?" the employee asked, pointing down the hall.

"Yes."

"He is lucky man."

June blushed.

"Where you are from?"

"Wisconsin."

He wrinkled his eyebrows. "You speak Spanish?"

She shook her head.

"Little?" He held two fingers close together and squinted, questioning, teasing.

"*Vamos a la discoteca*," June said. She shrugged her shoulders apologetically.

The man laughed. "*Sí, vamos a la discoteca.* We dance!" He grabbed her by the waist, holding one arm in the air and clasping his hand around hers. As they moved, June could feel the warmth from his soft stomach against hers. He hummed softly and pulled her around. She breathed in his powdery scent as their inner thighs rubbed over each other, as he turned them and hummed. And then he stopped, dropping her hands, laughing.

"I dance with you anytime," he said.

June was beaming. She could feel the heat in her face.

"Okay," she said.

"Okay. *Bueno.*" He reached to her hand dangling at her side and squeezed it. "Shoon," he said.

She did not run into him the whole next day. She told Harvey she wasn't feeling well—just a headache—and that he should again go bird-watching without her. But she wanted to look for the hotel employee. She just wanted to see him at least, even if they didn't talk.

She sat in the lobby for hours, but he didn't appear once. Another couple, traveling from Australia, checked in, but someone else helped them with their bags.

By dinner, she felt mopey. There was a new forcefulness in her annoyance when Harvey returned sopping wet, raving about birds. He was so busy bopping around, jotting notes in his journal and making sketches, walking away from the page and squinting down to check their accuracy, as if he were a real artist, that he didn't even ask how she was feeling. June sat on the bed flooded with irritation, not quite sure where so much of it had come from all at once. She remembered screaming the other night that she wanted to leave. At the time, she had meant Panama. Now if she were to say it, she thought she would mean him. Just like that.

Later, at dinner, the hotel employee was again diagonal from her at the table. He said, "Shoon," cordially, nodding at her. Harvey laughed at him, and June eyed Harvey angrily.

Harvey kept his arm around her until the food came, though he wasn't looking at her. He was again talking with the German next to him. She was an armrest, sitting silently at a table. She glanced now and then at the hotel employee, but he gave away nothing. Finally, between spoonfuls of rice pudding at dessert, she asked him, "What's your name?"

"Diego," he answered. And then he stared at her, it seemed, for a whole minute, even after she had gone back to eating.

It would have been easier, weeks later when she was back at home, if she had been able to convince herself that she was up in the middle of the night trying to find ice and she had run into him. Or that she and Harvey had gotten into a terrible fight and she had walked out of their room in a fury, slamming the door behind her, forgetting she didn't have a key. But the truth was that she went willingly, eagerly. That night after Harvey was asleep in his bed, June re-dressed and padded down the dark hallway. She knocked on Diego's door and woke him. She was praying he wouldn't ask how she had found him, because she didn't want to admit that she had followed him after dinner that night to a different part of the hotel, where a few of the employees stayed during the week.

When he opened the door, he was wearing athletic shorts and a white undershirt. He said, "You are lost?"

It was such a simple question.

"Yes," she said.

"I take you back," he said. He started to close the door behind him and step out into the hall.

June threw her hands on his chest and said, "No."

He appeared startled.

"There is problem?" he asked. "With your room? I get the manager."

She felt frustrated. She wanted him to understand her, why she had come. This was the sort of thing she would never do and now that she was doing it, she wanted it to go perfectly, to go better than this.

"Can I come in?" she asked finally.

"Yes. Please," he said, and opened the door for her.

The room was decidedly small but very neat. He patted the bed and invited her to sit.

He stood in front of her, his back against the wall. Neither of them said anything. Enormous, bloated minutes passed and then Diego stepped toward her and took her hands in his. She was crying. She felt so foolish. He wiped her cheek with his thumb.

"You miss something?" he said.

"I'm okay," she lied.

He smiled. "I see all the time. The guests get sad. They miss their home."

"I just thought it would be different from this."

"Panama?"

"No. Panama is very nice."

Diego nodded.

"The trip," June said. "I thought the trip would be different."

"What it was you wanted?"

"I wanted it to be romantic." June knew she shouldn't have said that. She knew it sounded too much like an invitation. But wasn't that what she was doing here, in his room?

Diego leaned down and kissed her. June could smell his cologne. When they pulled apart, she wondered, briefly, if this happened to him often. If he danced with all the tourists in the hallway and kissed them in his room at night. But then he said, "I'm sorry. Has been a very long time for me." And she felt a hazy sense of relief.

They stared at each other for a while. June was amazed at how much she wanted Diego to kiss her again. But he didn't. He said once more, "I'm sorry."

June stood. "Will I see you tomorrow?" she asked.

"Tomorrow? No. I go home then." He told her that he lived in a place called El Rompío and that he had an aunt there and two dogs. He took a bus on the weekends to see them. He explained that a weekend staff person would come and would need his hotel room.

When he said it, when she realized that she would not be able to sneak to his room again tomorrow night to see him as she surely would have, something caught in her throat. "What time?" she asked.

"The bus come at three o'clock," he told her.

It had taken everything June had to walk back to her room, but she had done it. She replayed the encounter in her head all the way back to her room. Harvey was snoring lightly when she opened the door and climbed into her bed. The rain pattered on the metal roof, though she hardly heard it.

The guide was leading them to Pipeline Road. This was the exact place, supposedly, where a world record number of birds had been spotted. Every so often Raul Sanchez de Arenas would stop and point to something

in a tree. Harvey would look quickly through his binoculars and then murmur, nod. The first few times, he
offered the binoculars to June, too, but she always
shook her head and by now Harvey had stopped offering. The humidity was oppressive. It was still raining
but under the umbrella of tree leaves only sprinkles
spit through. June hung back, staring at the footprints
she made in the mud with her galoshes. She had come
out today because she felt guilty about last night. It was
the only reason. She never saw what Harvey saw. A blur
of color darting through the air. A speck of something
unknowable in a tree. It was a mystery to her. But on
the trail, all she could think of was Diego, when she
would see him again, how she could possibly see him
before he got on the bus today.

June suctioned her galoshes out of the mud when
she heard Harvey calling her name. She walked toward
him. When she caught up, she learned that Raul had
arranged for them to take a small boat across the river,
toward the canal. She wanted to tell them that her socks
were soaked or claim again that she wasn't feeling well
so that she could leave and go back to the hotel.

But Harvey kept repeating "The Panama Canal! It's
the eighth wonder of the world, June!" and it was clear
that he wasn't going to let her miss it.

She followed Harvey and Raul through the dense
thicket of trunks and fronds, everything rich with

greens and browns. Small, colorful frogs clung to twigs. The tinny sounds of the rain forest echoed around her.

There was only one life vest when they got to the boat. Raul handed it to June even though Harvey tried to grab it first.

"Only a precaution," Raul assured him.

June's bright orange poncho stuck out like wings under the bulky vest. The boat, a small, wooden, canoe-type contraption, pulled away from the shore. June was quiet, seated on a wooden plank, cupping her kneecaps with her hands, squeezing them as if she were trying to break through the skin with her fingertips. She could feel the rain now that they were out on the open water. It screamed down, stung her skin. The river was choppy and rough. The front of the boat skated up waves and slapped down against the surface. Again and again. Raul steered the boat into them head-on.

June said, "I've never seen waves like this on a river."

"Not waves, just the water moving," Raul said, and clapped his hands to imitate their motion.

But whatever they were, they were more than glorified ripples, the spine of each cresting with foam. June felt a little sick but she wasn't sure it was because of the motion. The boat struggled farther from the shore.

Raul looked back from his post and shouted, "This is fun, no!"

The boat rolled to the side and Raul turned back quickly to straighten it. Harvey gripped the plank where he sat. June wondered if, in his life, Harvey had ever had this little control over anything, if he knew what it was to be tossed and rocked by something out of your hands, if he had ever experienced smallness.

A patchwork of lightning flared in the sky.

"Can I have your life vest?" Harvey asked. His face was pale.

"What?"

"June! You know I can't swim. Please!"

A bird swooped overhead.

Harvey loosened his hands from the plank and raised his binoculars. "What was that?" he asked.

June looked off to her side, feeling the churning of the water under her. She saw, through a lilac haze, enormous ships lined up to pass through the canal.

"A swift," June heard Raul reply.

"A white-collared swift?" Harvey asked.

June sighed. She took off her life vest and laid it on the damp floor of the boat by Harvey's feet. Harvey would see it when he stopped peering at the bird for long enough. How many times had she wanted to tell him: Stop looking up. Look at me! He still had his head tilted back at the sky when she jumped. The water, disarmingly warm, smacked against her. She started swimming

instantly. The waves jerked her back a little each time
she moved forward.

She didn't look back but she heard Raul shouting
and she assumed he had jumped in after her by now.
She pulled hard with her arms, digging through the
water, swimming toward the shore, toward the hotel.
She felt the best she ever had, a feeling she would never
be able to explain to anyone, not to Harvey who, tomorrow on the airplane, would keep asking her over and over
why she had done it; not to Diego who would smile
warmly when he saw her drenched. She swam without
knowing what would come next, the rain shooting down,
her poncho floating like silk under the water, her body
fighting to get her to the shore. And while she fought, she
finally understood something about Harvey—what it
meant to him to chase something like a bird, something
graspable but beyond your grasp, something fluttering
in the distance, something surprising and new and rare.

THE WIDE, PALE OCEAN

It was after church on a Sunday in February that the priest asked my mother if she would like to be Mary in the Easter procession that year.

"Virgin or Magdalene?" she said.

"*La virgen*," Father Castillo replied, and a fierce smile lit up my mother's face. She looked down at me and raised her eyebrows and nodded as if to say, See, Ysabel? See what your mother can do?

"There is a rehearsal the week before," Father Castillo continued, "and you will be required to make your own costume." Father Castillo used to preside over a church in Panama City. He was new to this area, so I don't think he knew what he was getting into by extending this invitation to my mother. He was dressed in white robes and clutched a black binder to his chest like armor.

"Excellent," my mother said. She was trying to remain composed, but I could tell she was ready to burst from happiness.

"Yes, it is God's work." Father Castillo clasped both of his hands around one of my mother's and gave it a firm shake to signal that the conversation was over. He patted my shoulder as we walked out, and asked us to keep Jesus in our hearts.

My mother pointed her index finger at her chest. "He's right here, Father!" she shouted, smiling like her face was going to split in two.

We lived on a small island called Taboga, where the handful of streets that existed were little more than winding stone paths and the only motorized vehicles were the boats from the city that docked at our pier on the weekends. Sherbet-colored houses with red roofs rose like steep mountain faces along the sides of the streets, built on wooden support beams that held them up and away from the water that ruffled in when the beach flooded, as it sometimes did during the rainy season. Some of the houses had been converted into tiny stores that sold groceries and bath products and hardware, and two with balconies had been turned into small restaurants. A white church stood in the middle of the town, with a clearing in front for community gatherings or for street vendors to sell their wares. Wispy palm trees towered over everything, and dark green tropical plants as well as vibrant flowers crowded the ground. Through it all, animals—mostly dogs but also frogs, iguanas, and a few peacocks—roamed lethargically, as if we humans were visitors in their space.

It was all I could do to stop my mother from skipping the whole way home. She kept bouncing ahead and turning around, walking backward in front of me while she shook my arms.

"Imagine! Me! In a parade."

I smiled. "I know, Mami."

"Everyone will see me."

I said, "I bet the real Virgin Mary wasn't even this excited when she found out she was having the baby Jesus."

My mother frowned. "The real Virgin Mary?" she said, as if she had forgotten that the real Virgin Mary was not her. But the frown slid away in an instant, and her eyes flashed once again as she said, "*Ay Dios!* What will I wear?"

I was born underwater in a bathtub at our local hotel. My mother had never liked doctors and chose instead to have a midwife. That's what she told me. The midwife insisted the birthing process would be easier in a tub. There was nothing more than a standing shower at our house, just a pipe coming through a wall, so my mother reserved a room at the only hotel on the island—the most money she ever spent at one time in her life, she said—and checked in as soon as she went into labor. She walked to the hotel from our house when she first started feeling the contractions course through her. Her water broke and splashed down her legs and soaked her shoes on the way there. The midwife met her in room 221. Seven hours later, I came out, under the water, and the midwife pulled me up into the air.

My father was back in the city, unaware that he was my father at all. He was simply a man my mother slept with once when he came to the island with his friends for the afternoon. His name was Ronaldo and he was better at the merengue than the tango, but that was all I knew. I used to press my mother for more, but she always maintained it was not important. When we took the ferry to the city to do our shopping, sometimes I had the urge to tap every man I saw on the shoulder and ask whether his name was Ronaldo, whether he had gone to Taboga with his friends for an afternoon fifteen years ago, whether he had slept with a girl named Gabriella, who had a lone freckle under her right eye. Sometimes I thought I could find him that way.

My mother and I lived in a faded green house

perched one story above ground level. It was a big, open space, like a dance hall with a few rooms at either end. Linoleum tiles covered the floor except where there was a single navy bath rug my mother had placed by the door to welcome visitors, which in reality meant clients, coming to pick up their clothes and linens from my mother, who was the seamstress on the island. A brown chenille couch that my mother had reupholstered herself was pushed against one wall and across from it stood an undersized television set on a table with gilded S-shaped legs. The kitchen was small, the cabinets browned with steam and grease from so many years of cooking. Then there was the bedroom, which my mother and I shared. Once in a while, when it was too hot to be so near each other, one of us would sleep on the couch, but otherwise we slept side by side every night, the fan blowing over us, the milk-and-rose scent of my mother's night cream settled into the sheets. A line of windows stretched all the way around our house and we kept them open even when it was raining because my mother was adamant about being able to hear the gentle brushing of the ocean any time of day.

I was on summer break so my mother asked me to help her with her costume. We hadn't been home ten minutes and already she was pulling out paper, a pen, her sewing machine, pins, a measuring tape, a white marking pencil, a thimble, two spools of thread, the kitchen chair, and a pair of scissors.

"Why did you bring the chair?" I asked, pointing to its rusted metal frame and padded orange seat covers.

"So I can stand on it and you can measure me."

"Why can't I measure you on the box?" My mother had a wooden box her clients usually stood on to get measured.

"It's more professional this way."

She seemed to have her mind made up about this since she was climbing onto the chair already and offering me the measuring tape, as if she were holding onto the tail of a snake.

She told me to measure her hips, her bust, her waist, her head. She smiled when I reported the numbers.

"Those women at the beach, they try to be too thin. You should want to be like this, Ysabel. Full." She swayed her hips a little and winked at me.

"Okay, Mami."

I was getting anxious to leave. I should have gone straight from Mass but I knew my mother wouldn't let me get away that fast. She needed someone to share her excitement with, at least for a little while. I was supposed to be at the soccer field to meet Lucho Morales, a boy from my school. I had seen him a few days earlier and he said he needed to talk to me. I tried to ask him, About what? But he wouldn't say. He just told me to meet him Sunday by the field.

"Okay, help me down," my mother said. She reached her hands to me.

I took them and delivered her safely to the floor.

"What did the Virgin Mary wear?" I asked.

"Robes. Blue robes, I think. But that doesn't sound very flattering, does it?" my mother said, and I could see then where this was headed.

"But if that's what she wore, then you have to wear it, too. You have to dress like she did."

"You think?"

"You're supposed to be her."

"But I could still be her in nicer clothes, no?"

"Why don't you ask Father Castillo?"

"Bah," she said. "You'll see. I'm going to look radiant."

My mother was always my true love. Since the beginning, it's been just the two of us. Her parents died in a plane crash when she was sixteen. They were on their way to Venezuela to visit her father's cousin. It was why she could get on a boat to go to Panama City when the need arose, but she refused to entertain thoughts of going anywhere that required flying. A few women from the island went to Miami once and told everyone about it when they got back. My mother said she didn't want to hear their stories, and when someone asked her why, she said because she would never go and that was a fact. She didn't say anything about not flying, but I knew that was the reason. Panama is all I need, she told the women.

When I was little, my mother and I were almost inseparable. At parties, when other kids would run off and play among themselves, I stayed attached to my mother like a growth, hugging my arms around her thigh like I would die if I let go. She never tried to shoo me off. I remember for about a year she wore these lavender velvet pants, which I loved because they were the softest against my face as she dragged me along everywhere. For a long time, I never even thought it was strange that I didn't have a father to speak of. My mother was simply everything. I was hardly aware that something was missing. And I knew that she needed me, too.

When I got a little older, we would go to the beach together. Sometimes, when my mother was feeling ambitious, we would sneak onto the hotel beach, which normally was only for guests. The hotel beach was a cordoned-off boomerang of sand that swung around the corner of the island. To keep the sand fine and smooth, men went out every day and swept it with wide brooms that looked like giant mustaches. My mother always rented a standing umbrella from the countless men hawking them to all the pale tourists who might truly need one. We lay under it, our bodies directly on the sand because my mother saw no need for towels. Why put anything between herself and God's earth? she would say.

When she got hot enough, she went to the edge of the water and sat with her legs outstretched, letting the foam glide over her ankles and up her thighs, her body sinking in the wet sand. I watched her from under the umbrella, the U-shaped back of her red bathing suit bright in the sun, her hair pulled up off her neck.

She taught me how to float. Like a dead man, she said. Without cares. She walked me into the water and we would draw a deep breath and duck under, casting limply on the current until we had to come up for air. She used to hold my hand when we went under because she knew I was scared. After the first few times, though, she let go and we floated side by side.

I was out of breath by the time I reached the soccer field. On the scorched and matted grass, two boys used an empty milk jug as a ball, kicking it with their bare feet. I still had on my church clothes—a white eyelet skirt and an orange blouse—because I hadn't had time to change. I saw Lucho sitting on a bench. In the sunlight, his skin was smooth like a caramel candy. I had prayed so hard at church that morning that he wanted to talk to me to tell me he liked me and I was nervous now thinking about it.

"Hi," I said when I got to the bench.

He looked up, squinting against the sun, and then stood. "This is so stupid," he said.

"It's okay." I held my tongue between my teeth.

He sighed. "Javi wants to know if you would kiss him."

Javier was Lucho's best friend. I felt something enormous shift in my chest like a landslide.

"Javi?"

"He says he's been dreaming about it since school last year."

I tried to imagine it, but Javier had dry lips that made it hard to envision.

"Why doesn't he ask me himself?"

Lucho shrugged. "Scared, I guess."

Part of me was thrilled that any boy would want to kiss me and that he would be too scared—of me!—to ask. But how I wished it were Lucho instead.

"I've never done it before," I admitted quietly.

Lucho looked amused. He raised his forearm to his mouth and kissed it. "It's like this," he said.

"But on the lips?"

"Pretty much the same."

I nodded and looked down at my flat white sandals. Silence gathered in the space between us until, the next thing I knew, Lucho grabbed my shoulders and his lips, soft as pudding, touched mine for an instant. He stepped back quickly. "It's like that," he said.

"No," I said.

"No what?"

"You have to tell Javi no."

"Why not? You were all right."

I was breathing fast. "I like you, Lucho," I said.

"You joking?" he asked.

"No."

I was trying so hard to read his face but I couldn't tell what he was thinking. He just kept staring at me. The boys on the soccer field shrieked as one of them scored.

"Okay," he said finally, and he grinned. "Javi's gonna be mad, though."

Things quickly became tense. Lucho and I had to meet in secret, because of Javi and because of my mother. My mother started complaining that she never saw me anymore. She worked from our house during the day, mending and altering piles of clothes. Usually I was responsible for picking up stray straight pins from the floor and returning them to their cushion. She told me she had stepped on six in the past week and showed me, on the soles of her feet, the spots where the blood had beaded up and dried, a constellation of scabs.

"I'm sorry, Mami," I said.

"Where is it you go anyway?"

"Just around."

"You got tired of me?"

"No."

I hadn't told her anything about Lucho because I knew she would say I was too young for a boy. Or that no boy was good enough for me. Or that trying to keep a boy wasn't worth it. Or any number of protestations.

"You come back so late," my mother said. She'd turned back to the sewing machine and said it quietly.

"But I always come back."

"Mmmmm." She pushed a piece of green fabric through the machine.

I stayed at home that day, though it felt like the hardest thing I would ever do. I called Lucho and told him my mother needed me. He said he did, too, which was the first time he had said anything like that to me and my chest squeezed the life out of my heart when I heard it. Tomorrow, I told him. But I was pulled in two by the thought of him waiting for me and by the sight of my mother, alone at her machine, missing me.

I picked the straight pins off the floor and swept up the fabric ends and loose threads. The day was cloudy, casting a gray veil over our house and inside it, too. That night, I lay on my back on the bed while my mother rubbed on her night cream and then came to bed. Usually, she hummed as she got ready for bed, but that night she was quiet. When she lay down, the thin mattress sighed and sagged beneath her as she squirmed into place. My eyes were open and I stared at the bands of moonlight stretched across our stucco ceiling like tiny highways, like the ones they had in the city. After a few minutes, I turned on my side, wriggling toward my mother until I could get my head in the crook of her shoulder, pulling her arm over me like a blanket. I was trying to see what it would feel like if I lay next to Lucho. I knew my mother probably thought I wanted to be close to her—and in a way I did—but I was also imagining him.

Lucho and I found our favorite spot, among the trees, as far from the town as we could manage. At first, we sat on the ground with our fingers laced through each other's, gossiping about people in school because we were nervous and didn't know what else to talk about. We tried to climb the trees but the delicate trunks shredded beneath our feet, which we knew they would since we had both lived here forever, but it was a period of acting like we didn't know things we did just to be able to experience them together, as if for the first time. On the other side of the island, where no one I knew had ever been, thousands of brown pelicans were supposedly making a home, the shoreline thick with them. We walked as far as we could without getting lost and held our breath and strained to hear them but we never could. We kissed a lot, under the midday sun, pretending we were in the *telenovelas* sometimes and other times letting our lips meet while the rest of our bodies stayed rigid and unsure, afraid to do anything but peck at each other like birds. And then, after almost three weeks, Lucho put his hand under my shirt.

"Have you ever done this before?" I asked when his hand was still only making circles on my stomach. I knew where he was going.

"No," he said. "Don't tell anyone that, though." He smiled.

I lay back and let him do it, to see how it would feel. He was slow but finally his hand reached my breast. I wished it was bigger, something more than a little lump, but it wasn't yet. He dropped his hand over me like a clamshell and kept it still.

"How does that feel?" he asked.

It didn't feel like much. "Okay."

"Should I press down?" he asked. I had my eyes closed and I could feel the heat from the sun on my skin where my shirt was raised.

"Try it," I said.

He flattened his palm and rubbed it against me. After a few seconds he stopped and drew his hand away. I opened my eyes and tugged my shirt down over my stomach. "That was good," I told him.

I tried to come home early in the evenings, to spend time with my mother before she went to bed. Often, by the time I walked through the door, though, she was already asleep and snoring lightly with her face half-buried in her pillow. One time I leaned down to kiss her good night on her forehead and, with the hand I put down on the pillow to steady myself, I felt something damp. I ran my fingertips over the spot and I knew—she had been crying. I began running my hand over her pillowcase every time she was already sleeping and usually I could feel the moisture, her collected tears.

Once—only once—she was waiting for me when I came home after she would normally have been in bed.

"It's so late," she said. She was standing with her arms crossed, her back to our floor fan, which whirred and snapped behind her as it turned. She wore her nightgown and nightcap, and the skin under her eyes had a gray-violet cast without her makeup.

"Where have you been?" she asked.

I shrugged.

"Something happened to your brain? You can't remember where you just were?"

"I wasn't doing anything wrong," I said, which probably made it sound more like I was.

"Get in the shower," she said.

"What?"

"Whatever it is you've been doing, I want you to wash it off."

"But it was nothing."

"Why can't you do nothing here at home then?" She raised her voice.

"Because."

Her eyes were wide. She was hardly blinking. "Because?"

"I don't know."

"Come on. I'll turn on the water. You can keep your clothes on if that's easier." She started past me, toward the bathroom.

"I can do what I want," I said, though in truth I was scared to say it.

"Is that what you think?"

I was afraid even to nod. My mother's nostrils flared and her eyes flashed. I don't think I had ever seen her so shakingly angry.

"Because that's wrong," she picked up, after a few seconds. "I decide what you do. I choose where you can go. I choose who you spend time with. It's always been that way." Each time she said "I" she jabbed her index finger against her breastbone, so hard I thought it might go through.

I shook my head. To this day, I don't know where I came up with the strength to do it, but I said, "No, Mami. *I* can choose."

"Why don't you choose *me* anymore?" she screamed, a high watery scream that smothered every bit of silence in the world.

I gazed at the floor. I knew what she was thinking— that I was all she had in the world and that I was leaving her. It had always been the two of us and now it wasn't. "I don't know," I said softly.

We both stood there.

"You should take a shower," my mother said finally, and then turned from me and walked to the bedroom.

There were times when I needed to be on my own, too—away from Lucho, away from my mother, away from the world. I started doing what I had often done when I was young: wading into the ocean and holding my breath underwater. I stood on the beach and watched as the water lapped up on the sand, darkening it, the moisture spreading out, as if the shoreline were a piece of paper whose edge was dipped in water. Eventually, I would walk out, the water wrapping around my ankles and then my knees and then my waist as I made my way deeper. After a certain point, the sand stopped being rough, studded with broken shells, and instead became like velvet under my feet. When the water was up to my shoulders, I drew as much air as I could get into my lungs and went under. I loosed my feet from the sand and floated. I stayed as still as I could. The sounds of the island were muffled, almost nonexistent. I had learned long ago not to open my eyes because of the salt, but I could see myself: weightless and wilted, swaying like seaweed under the current of the water. Back and forth. I stayed for as long as I could and then slipped my head through the surface of the water to get air. Almost always, I came up meters from where I had started, tugged by the water. I never went down twice in a row even though I loved being under. I saved it for the next time: that feeling, just for a moment, like I needed nothing and no one needed me, like I had lost myself, like I was lost to the world.

Life went on like this until Easter. Lucho and I took every opportunity to scurry into the hills of the island and be alone. Back in school, I had been attracted to him because he was good-looking—his hair not as black as the other boys', slightly blanched from the sun; his skin smoother, almost creamy; his legs not as skinny

as some of his friends'. But I was learning of his kind-
ness and of a certain shyness that lurked beneath a
veneer of confidence. It was easy to talk to him. Each
time I touched him, it was as if a live wire was switching
under my skin. I even told him about my father. Out of
embarrassment, I had always lied to my friends and said
that my father died soon after I was born. I thought it
would be too humiliating to admit that my father was a
man my mother slept with once, a man my mother
hadn't known then and neither of us knew now. But it
felt okay when I told Lucho. He didn't say anything
back but he didn't judge either. He just smiled and
folded me in his arms.

I helped my mother with her costume, a more
ostentatious version of *La Virgen*'s humble blue-and-
white robes. We affixed sequins to every hem and lined
the cape and hood drape in pink satin. We also put
pleats around the back of the cape so it would billow
out in the wind during the procession, making the lining visible. She was very pleased with it when it was
finished.

"This is my big day," she said as soon as we woke up
on Easter morning. The white sunlight streamed
through our windows as if somewhere a dam had broken and sent it gushing forth. The thready chirping of
birds and the sound of dogs barking pierced the air outside. My mother was sitting straight up in our bed,

strands of her dark hair falling from under her night-cap. "Mass is at nine o'clock," she said, "and the procession is right after. I want you at both."

"I know."

"No running off doing whatever it is you have been doing."

"Okay." I rubbed my eyes. I could hardly keep them open in the sunlight.

Since that one night, my mother had never again confronted me about my activities apart from her, but she couldn't resist taking jabs when she had the chance. She slapped my thigh lightly through the sheet and made a tsk-ing sound with her mouth. "Get up," she said, and then stood and walked to the bathroom.

For me, Mass was just something to sit through. I wasn't like my mother, who was reverent and wide-eyed all the way through and who, when Father Castillo raised the cup of wine and the piece of bread to change them into blood and body, positively trembled with awe. The church was more lavishly decorated than usual, with mountains of flowers—orange and white, yellow and pink—clumped together in pots wrapped in colored foil. The scent was powerfully sweet and I spent the hour with my eyes closed, imagining I was in the hills with Lucho where, sometimes, when the temperature was just right, the fragrance from the flowers outside lifted in the same way. At the end of Mass, when

Father Castillo made the announcement about the Easter procession to follow, my mother squeezed my hand.

"I have to get ready!" she whispered, and quickly kissed both my cheeks before scampering down the aisle to the sacristy, where her costume awaited.

Lucho stood next to me during the procession. I had asked him to join me. Despite the risk that Javi might see us together, Lucho said he would come. He knew it was important to me. We watched as children in their Sunday clothes walked behind a man carrying a simple wooden cross, two planks bound at their intersection by rope. Then there was a break and for at least a minute nothing happened.

"Is it over?" Lucho asked.

"Wait," I said, craning my neck to see past the crowd of onlookers, and down the street.

Then the bells started. Many of the people lining the street had bells in their hands and, upon some cue that I had missed, they all started ringing them at once. It was a joyous, buoyant chorus, the sound of rays of sunlight breaking upon the earth. They started just as the rest of the procession came into view: Father Castillo carrying a carved wooden figure of Christ on the cross, maybe fifty people behind him walking with lit candles, little girls carrying bouquets of white flowers and, finally, my mother, waving at the crowd, smiling brightly. Everyone else was simply walking but my mother turned and bowed and waved so hard I could have sworn she was trying to shake her hand from her arm.

Lucho poked me and pointed at her. "What's she doing?"

I shrugged. "She's happy." But I wanted to bury my face in his arm from embarrassment. And I did turn away for a moment, to check the expressions on other people's faces and to stare briefly at my shoes as my mother passed in front of us.

"She tried to say something to you," Lucho said, poking me again.

I looked up then and waved. She was glancing back at me and I saw it in her eyes—a flicker of disappointment that I hadn't been watching her steadfastly the entire time. That's what she wanted: my whole attention always, my unwavering gaze. I saw her glance at Lucho, too, and I knew she disapproved. At that, I linked my arm through his and held it tight as my mother stared back at the two of us while she walked away, following the parade. As soon as she turned her head, I dropped Lucho's arm.

"Why didn't you tell me she was so close?" I asked accusingly. "I almost missed her."

"You knew she was there."

"You should have told me."

I didn't know why, but I was suddenly angry with him.

"Whatever, Ysabel," he said, shaking his head. He tried to take my hand once but I wouldn't let him. I felt so confused, everything bursting and crumbling inside of me. The town square erupted in celebration as the end of the procession snaked its way behind the church and out of sight. Lucho and I stood silent in the middle of the exuberance.

Finally he said, "Do you want to go?"

"I want to find my mother first," I told him.

"Really?"

I nodded.

"Okay. I'll wait for you, then," he said, and I knew he meant in our usual spot, where he would be kicking at rocks and drawing figures in the dirt until I arrived.

I didn't say anything back. I just started walking, navigating my way through the crowd, people clapping and singing and shouting over each other. When I got to the back of the church, Father Castillo was there carrying the tapered white candles in a fold of newspaper. He smiled when he saw me.

"Have you seen my mother?" I asked.

"She was a beautiful Virgin Mary."

"Do you know where she went?" I felt impatient.

"Down to the water, I think. Are you all right?" He shifted the candles in his arms.

"Thank you," I said, and started toward the beach.

As soon as I got there, I saw her. I saw the back of her, still in her costume, her ankles in the water. The blue satin swelled in the breeze. Then I watched as she walked deeper and deeper into the water, like she was sinking into the earth. Her cape clung to the surface until it grew soaked and slumped under. Finally she drew her head below the water. I kicked off my sandals and ran, as fast as I could, my feet burning on the hot, dry sand. I splashed into the water to where she was and dropped under. I knew, since she was the one who had taught me, that her eyes would be closed. I reached out my hand until I felt her, and I didn't let go. After just a few seconds, my lungs grew fuzzy with fire, tiny starbursts of pain popping in my chest. Even so, I held on. Lucho was somewhere in the white-hot sun waiting for me. I would find him later and for the whole summer we would go on as we had been, meeting in secret, exploring each other's skin, figuring out what it meant to be with another person. We would have silly conversations—about radio stations and hens and the restaurants in Panama City— that felt significant, and we would laugh over nothing, over one of us tripping on a branch or over a leaf stuck to my face. It would be like that until school started again, when he would tell me, for fear of losing Javi as a best friend, that we were finished. I would argue and say we could still meet in secret, that no one would know.

But Lucho was firm. He said that Javi and he always hung out after school so there would be no time for me, anyway. I would suffer for months and know for the first time the feeling of my heart breaking. I would know what my mother had been feeling for weeks. And I would discover how much of life is defined by what you want to keep and what you are forced to lose. But all of that would come later. Right then I was floating, holding my mother's hand. It was almost like flying. And I had the most beautiful image: I saw us from above, from the sky, two flecks of being connected at the edge of the wide, pale ocean, lost to everything but each other.

THE BOX HOUSE
AND THE SNOW

Their house was a box. It was a perfect house. It was the father's favorite thing in the world. No one else he knew had a house quite like it and no one, he thought, ever would again. It was the sort of place that should go on the National Register of Best Houses, if such a thing existed. And if it didn't exist, it should be invented to honor this one house.

They lived in a valley between two mountains. There were forty-two other houses in their modest valley town. There were once forty-three other houses, but a few years earlier a whipping windstorm had its way with one of them and toppled it into a pile of matchsticks and glass. The man whose house had fallen had built the house himself, a feat he often boasted of at length to everyone in the town. So when it crumbled, though they were nothing but kind and supportive to his face, the people in the town whispered behind the man's back about how embarrassing it was that the house had collapsed like a bad soufflé, and they laughed with derision and agreed that the man's pridefulness had been met with just punishment. The father was among those whispering and laughing and agreeing, though it scared him to recognize a bit of himself in the man, since the father, too, was buoyed by pride. But when he confessed this fear to his wife, she assured him that there was a difference between arrogant pride and joyous pride, and that the father possessed the latter, which was the acceptable variety. The father felt better. He even hired a photographer to take a picture of him and his wife and their daughter in front of their perfect house, to commemorate his joyous pride.

The valley town was huddled in the middle of a tropical country. The people there were used to air that never dropped below eighty degrees, air that was sticky and warm every year of their lives. So they were more than a little surprised when, one April morning, they encountered a curious white substance covering nearly everything they could see. The substance was snow.

Later, this is the story they would collectively decide upon, the legend they would pass down to their children and their children's children: The snowstorm came at night while everyone was sleeping. The world was perfectly still. No breeze rustling the trees; no whispers ribboning through the air; no animals yawning; no people turning in their sleep, flinching from their dreams; no soft gurgling in the sewers below the streets. The moon was masked behind thick clouds. The world was black, caked on and opaque. Then, all at once, millions of snowflakes burst from the murky sky and fluttered to the earth. It was a pillow ripping open. It was a silent, exploding firework. It was as if God had been collecting mounds and fistfuls and armfuls of snow for centuries and, finally, could hold the white flakes no more. He tore a seam in the fabric of heaven and sent the snowflakes scampering forth. At first, the snow danced through the air doing cartwheels, doing flip-flops, doing triple full twists and Arabian front tucks. Later, carried by a new wind, it leapt in great tumbling clumps like paratroopers. As the night went on, it shot down in a nosedive, in a fury, as if thrust from the sky against its will, as if spit from the mouths of angels. And later still, in a last heroic push before the sun came up in the morning, the snow grew so dense that it gave the appearance of cascading walls of snow, a world made from snow, solid all the way through. There was so much of it that the entire night sky was blanched, and the earth below it surrendered. The world turned white.

But before the people in the valley town settled upon this story, they had to deal with the astonishment of that morning. When they first woke their shutters were closed, as they were every night, to block out the blinding morning sun. There was a chill in the air stiffer than usual, but not enough to provoke alarm. It was not until, one by one, the people climbed out of bed and opened their doors that they noticed the snow. People plunged into the waist-high sea of white that flooded into their doorways. They looked out from their houses for their neighbors, for trees, for wire trash cans, for street signs—for anything familiar—but found that only the top half of everything was visible. Against houses and buildings, the snow soared, swept up gently by the wind like a cresting wave frozen in time.

The phones were quiet.

The electricity was severed.

The sewers were frozen.

Inside their houses, people talked on and on and on among themselves, in complete disbelief, trying to comprehend the world outside their windows.

In the perfect house, the father was the first one awake. He found himself pressed against his wife when he opened his eyes. He was shivering. For a moment, he believed he was sick. He groped for his watch on the bedside table and held it in front of him but, because of the perfect darkness in the house, he could not see the face. For a moment, he believed he had gone blind. He curled his icy toes around his wife's ankle. He smoothed the standing hairs on his arms. He stared into pitch-blackness and then became scared. His wife's ankle was as cold as his toes. For a moment, he believed he was dead.

When finally he got up, the father pulled three pairs of socks over his feet and padded to the front door, stealing his way through the dark. The iciness of the wrought-iron door handle shocked him but when he opened the door, slowly, pulling it toward him, what he saw shocked him more: a bright white earth that stretched for miles. The snow that had built up against the door gently tumbled into the house. The father tried to nudge it out with his toe and in doing so, made a soft indentation at the bottom of the snow wall. He stared at the glittering snowscape. He took a step back into the house and closed the door.

The mother felt the cold slink in through her pores and spread like a vapor under her skin. In the night, she thought it was a dream. She pulled a sheet over her body and fought her way into a ball, holding her knees to her chest to stay bunched. She slept restlessly, trembling. She knew something was not right.

And then the father poked her in the morning. He whispered, Get up.

It's the middle of the night, she told him. It's dark.

It's not dark. It's just that the windows are covered.

Well then open the shutters. You always open the shutters when you get up.

The shutters are open.

What do you mean? the mother asked, sighing.

You'll see, the father said. He pulled her out of her ball.

What's going on? she asked.

The father slid socks over her feet as she sat on the bed. She was growing impatient.

You won't believe it, he told her. Then he dragged her through the house, guiding her with his hand.

I can't see a thing, she said.

The father opened the door for her. Light streamed into the house. He gave a dramatic bow. See this, he said.

The snow was big news. Reporters from all over were clamoring to cover it, but the problem was that they couldn't get into the town because the roads were blocked. The networks that could afford to sent helicopters to hover over the town. The shots were incomparable. The earth smoothed over, soft shimmering dimpled mounds. One network from Chile was so desperate to cover the story—which was being hailed as a miracle on par with tears from the statue of the Virgin Mary—that they diverted their traffic copter to the valley town. The result was sixty-six traffic accidents in Santiago in one day—a sort of anti-miracle.

The people in the town, eager to be on television, worked hard to clear pathways for the reporters to make their way in. They cleared streets using pots, pans, cookie sheets, watering cans, bowls, plastic bags, shoes, pillowcases, and couch cushions—anything they could find. The work was hard. They weren't prepared. They safety-pinned towels around their thighs and around their torsos to help keep their bodies warm. They swirled blankets around their shoulders and clutched them at the front to keep them closed. They lit their stoves and took turns warming their reddened hands over the hissing blue flames. They picked up their phones for a dial tone—to call the stations and invite them in—but were greeted by silence on the other end. They pulled at their TV knobs, hoping to see themselves on the news, hoping to see a government emergency alert, but the TVs stayed asleep. They took photographs of the great white ocean that had swallowed them whole, forcing teeth-chattering smiles for the camera as they stood outside. Two enterprising families trampled on the snow, spelling out HOLA with their footprints, and this image, captured by the swarm of helicopters overhead, became the most famous of the miracle snow.

The father used a silver platter he and the mother had received for their wedding to push the snow aside, enough so he could walk out the door. The soles of his sandals stamped a pattern of diamonds on the white land as he walked. He stopped at his fence, an iron fence ornate with curlicues and swirls. Snow rested in the spaces of the design. The father poked his finger at the snow. It came loose like a cutout and fell quietly against the powder on the other side. But he had not ventured outside, as others had, for fun or novelty. The father turned and looked at his perfect house, ambushed by snow. He thought of the man whose house had blown down as punishment for his pride. The father told himself that if he could keep his house standing, it would be God's way of telling him he had a reasonable sort of pride, one for which he did not deserve to be punished. On the other hand, if something happened to the house, it would mean that the father was a sinner, since the wrong sort of pride was a sin. On top of that, there were the news cameras. If the house collapsed, almost everyone in the world would know it. Things were getting serious.

Inside, the father told the mother to gather dishrags and bath towels. The mother was sitting at the kitchen table with her knees pulled to her chest, trying to stay warm. She had checked on the daughter but let her keep sleeping. At this point, it seemed better than being awake. The mother raised her eyebrows as the father pointed to the wooden wall behind the sink.

Do you see how dark it is? he asked.

The mother turned to look. Something black blossomed in a patch above the sink.

It looks like a stain, she said.

It's water, the father said. It's seeping through.

But it rains here and the wood gets wet, the mother said.

The father shook his head. The snow is wrapped around the house like a boa constrictor. It's not the same as rain.

The mother was worried now but the father told her not to be. Get the dishrags and towels, he said. He showed her how to hold them up to the walls, how to use them to swab the water away.

The father woke the daughter next. Are you awake? he yelled. You have to get up! There's been a snowstorm, he said. He heard the daughter laugh from her room.

The father opened her bedroom door. It's true, he said.

But it doesn't snow here, the daughter argued.

I'm almost positive that's what it is. I've seen pictures before.

The daughter jumped up, giddy. Is it really? She rushed past the father to the front door. When she saw the snow, she shuddered and pulled her arms in through the sleeves of her nightgown. The air smelled like it had been laundered, fresh and wet. A bird sprang lightly into the snow, sinking in and flitting off again.

It's amazing, the daughter whispered.

Yes, okay, the father said, dragging her away from the door. That's enough of that. We need your help.

The father took a wooden chair from the kitchen and put it in what he estimated was the center of the house. Already the ceiling had begun to bow. The mother said she couldn't tell, but the father saw it. The roof was flat and the weight of the snow would collapse it.

The father told the daughter to put on her best socks and her warmest clothes. The mother, who could see what was coming next, protested. I'll stand on the chair myself, the mother said.

I've already taught you how to swab the walls, the father argued.

I'll teach the girl.

It will take too long. Someone needs to get on the chair now and that's the girl.

The mother bit her tongue.

The father told the daughter to stand on the chair.

No way, she said.

Do it or I'll bury you in that snow, the father shouted.

That's terrible, the mother said. Don't say that to her.

The father sighed. You're right. I'm feeling a little crazy. I'm sorry. *Please* get up on the chair.

The daughter put her arms back through her nightgown's armholes and climbed up wordlessly, her dark hair swimming down her back.

Reach your arms up, the father said. His expression was grave, his eyes wide and expectant.

The daughter did as he asked, gazing at the ceiling as her hands neared the wood.

Can you touch? the father asked.

The daughter flattened her palms against the ceiling.

The mother said, Are you okay?

The daughter said, I guess.

The father said, Now don't move.

Very slowly, small paths began to open up all over the town like arteries, allowing people to get around to most places, allowing life to flow again. The reporters gave round-the-clock updates and when by that evening not a single new snowflake had fallen, most of them packed up and left.

As far as the father knew, no one else's house had suffered. They all had sloped roofs so the snow tumbled off. For the first time, the father saw his own house as something less than perfect. It was not invincible. He complained about this to the mother.

But the mother said, This only proves it's *more* perfect than the rest. Because with this house comes a challenge. And surviving the challenge will only make you stronger. Do other people have houses that will make them stronger?

No, the father admitted, pleased by this logic. The father was also inspired by this logic. He went out and found one of the few news teams left in town and told them he had a knockout story for them. He promised them the greatest house in the world. The news team was about to leave the scene. There was only so much they could say about snow and only so much they could speculate about how it got there and what might happen next. But at the offer to see the greatest house in the world, they thought, Why not?

The news team arrived as the mother was squeezing rags over the sink. She was exhausted but the clay between the wood was softening so she had to work quickly. More than once, the mother had slumped in the corner and covered her face with one of the rags. She said a prayer, moving her lips against the terry cloth. She asked God to lift the snow, to suck it back into the sky. She imagined streamers of snow running up into the clouds. The dry earth would return to itself layer by layer.

The daughter stood, perched on the wooden kitchen chair in the middle of the floor, her arms spread and raised overhead, palms flat and pressed into the wet wood, fingers splayed. She watched her mother huddle in the corner. She heard whispering but could not make out the words. The daughter itched one ankle with the toes of her other foot. She wore red woolen knee-high socks that her mother had bought once to make into stockings for Christmas but never had. Then the daughter heard the commotion outside. Who's here? she said.

Who's where? the mother asked.

The daughter nodded her head toward the door.

The mother peered out and then shrieked.

At the sound of the shriek, the father looked up and strode to the house. Isn't it magnificent? he said, motioning toward the news team. Now everyone will know about our house. The whole world will be able to see it.

I'm not wearing any makeup, the mother said, and skittered to the bathroom.

The father peered outside at the crew and then looked to the daughter. Whatever you do, do not move, he said. Even after the snow melts, the wood will get heavy with water. You have to hold it up. The whole world will be watching.

The daughter sighed.

Don't sigh, the father scolded.

I don't think it will fall, the daughter said.

Do you really want to find out? the father asked.

Although the father had not foreseen it, the story ended up being not so much about the house as about the daughter standing inside the house, literally holding it together with her own two hands. The news team requested interviews with the daughter, but the father insisted that she not be bothered. She needed to focus. Sometimes, though, the daughter yelled out requests for food or pleas that someone trade places with her because she was growing tired, even though the father pinched her legs when she did because he didn't want her to make him seem like a cruel father in front of the whole world, as he kept saying.

Failing the opportunity to interview the daughter, the news anchor at least wanted to interview the father. The father welcomed the attention.

How much longer will the girl have to hold up the ceiling? the news anchor asked. She wore a pink suit. She was a gumdrop in the snow.

The snow has almost melted, the father replied.

Why can't we talk to her?

I already told you.

Tell me again.

If you start talking to her, she will be distracted. It's important for her to focus. She's holding up the most perfect house in the world.

Would a perfect house be capable of collapsing?

It won't collapse. You'll see.

Then the father flashed a huge smile at the camera, showing his gums.

Cut, the news anchor said.

Did you get a shot of the house? the father asked.

Sure, the news anchor replied.

When it was time for bed, the father told the daughter to stay on the chair.

All night? the daughter said. You have to be kidding.

All night, the father replied, and the daughter did as she was told.

The mother had trouble sleeping that first night. She kept dreaming she was wet. She kept feeling water edging under her skin, under her nails, into her ears. She would wake and touch her skin until she was sure it was dry, and then fall asleep, fitfully, again. She dreamed she was stuck underwater. She was submerged in a tank, floating in pale gray water. She was holding her breath but her lungs were losing air. She dreamed she was in the mouth of a volcano, buoyed by lava. She could feel the volcano rumbling beneath her. She could feel the vibrations traveling through her toes to her knees to her hips to her shoulders. And then the volcano exploded. She was thrown out. But what it spewed wasn't lava and ash. It was snow. And the mother landed facedown on the ground, snow raining over her. She tried to get up but she couldn't. The snow pushed her down like hundreds of tiny hands. She tried to open her mouth to scream but it was filled with the flakes. She dreamed she was choking on snow.

By the morning of the second day, the news team had grown bored even with the story of the girl. They packed up and left. The father learned this when he went out to bid them good morning. He was disappointed to see they had gone, but turned his attention again to the house. Conditions were better than yesterday. The sun was out and the father had managed to push the snow away from the house in a ring. The problem now was the rivulet of water surrounding the house. It would creep in at the baseboards, he knew. He would tell the mother where to concentrate her efforts today.

The daughter had been holding up the ceiling all night. Once, she bent her elbows the tiniest bit to see what would happen and she felt it: the ceiling began to give way. She re-straightened her arms. She knew then that the father was right: If she got down, the ceiling would fall. The house would be ruined. Her shoulders popped. Her wrists creaked under the weight, warning her in a language of aching—*please, we won't be able to take it much longer.* But the daughter had no choice.

When the father came back inside, the daughter asked for breakfast. The father sped past her, spoke to the mother, and sped back out again, into town.

Hey, the daughter yelled after him, but the father seemed not to hear.

In certain parts of town, the snow was melting fast, trickling along the edges of itself, running into sewers and soil and lower land. One woman's sandals, which she had left on her stoop the night before the storm, were washed away by the runoff, gliding down the street into an open manhole. Armed with a flashlight, her husband was underground for hours, searching for her shoes.

By nightfall tomorrow, the townspeople guessed, the snow would be gone. When the earth had had enough, there would be flooding, but it had flooded before and they would handle it as they always had.

After the father left, the mother went out, too. The father had warned her repeatedly that one of them needed to stay at the house at all times to keep an eye on the daughter. And besides, the mother was supposed to be swabbing away. But the mother was restless and lonely in the house and when the father left, she wanted to go out, too.

I'll be gone for a little while, she told the daughter.

Can I come? the daughter asked.

The mother shook her head. I'll get you something if you'd like, she said.

I'm tired.

I know. It can't be much longer now.

I'm so tired.

The mother patted the top of the daughter's foot. Just hold on a little longer. I'll bring you a bag of marzipan.

The daughter was too exhausted to argue. Satisfied, the mother walked out the door, her feet crunching against the packed powder.

There was no telling how long the mother and father had been gone. But the daughter started to come undone. By now, the ceiling had lost almost all the snow, but the wood—saturated with water, soaked through by the unexpected winter—was nearly blackened and heavy with melting. The weight climbed into the daughter's bones. Her eyelids fluttered. She could no longer feel her hands. Her stockinged toes curled over the edge of the chair and her heels throbbed. Blood swelled in her neck and pooled in her shoulders. Her hips were cast forward, locked under the weight. It was as if the roof were fighting her, intent on crashing to the ground. She was beyond the point of crying out. She thought she couldn't do it. She thought it was too much. But she told herself: One more second now, one more second now, now it's just one more second. Fighting to keep herself going. And then, somewhere near the end of the day, the daughter started crying. Tears poured from her eyes the way the snow had gushed from the sky days earlier. Her entire body wept, sobbing with anguish.

When the father came back from town, he was relieved to see the house still intact. But he was unrelieved when he walked into the house. The daughter was still on the chair, her head lolling forward. The father hardly saw her. What he noticed instead was the water around his ankles. All over the floor. A calm layer, almost ten centimeters deep, filled the house from wall to wall. The father waded through it silently, the soft swish of water the only sound.

The mother came home then, too, and stood in the open door, water sliding out over her feet.

It's ruined, the father said softly. The water got through somehow. She let it through.

It could have come from anywhere, the mother said.

No. Everything around the house is dry. It came from the ceiling. I knew if it bowed enough, it would splinter. The water would come through.

The ceiling is still perfectly flat, the mother said, glancing up at it.

You could never see it, the father said. He knelt and lapped his hands through the water. It's ruined, he said again.

It will dry, the mother said.

The father shook his head. The ceiling will have to be rebuilt. The whole house.

If the father had raised his hands to his mouth, he would have tasted the salt of the daughter's tears, but he didn't. He simply scooped the water over and over with his hands, his back rounded, his head sinking farther into his chest.

Some books are damaged, the mother said. Only things on the floor!

It's the wood, the father said. It's too wet now. The walls are too soft. They'll fall in soon. She let it through, he whispered.

The daughter, her slender arms strained under the weight of the house, her tears long since dry was too exhausted to speak. She simply stared at the father and held up the ceiling.

COME TOGETHER, FALL APART

Belief is believing in God;
faith is believing that God believes in you.
—Andre Dubus, "A Father's Story"

OCTOBER 23, 1989

We were all scared in those days. Noriega was on his
way to collapse and already the chaos had started.

Near the beginning of it all a homemade bomb
exploded near my Tía Reina's car while she was stopped
at a red light. It landed on the sedan next to her and
spit out like a firecracker, tearing through the passen-
ger side of her Toyota, crumbs of the fiery metal burning tiny holes through her skirt. She pushed herself out
of the car and rolled on the pavement until the fire was
smothered, leaving her with a band of burns across her
thighs like garter belts.

"Thank God it didn't get her face," her husband, Tito, said to the nurse at the hospital, as though there would be no use for a woman with a damaged face.

"She's very lucky," the nurse agreed, and left it at that.

I was fifteen then. Old enough to understand that the nurse meant lucky that it hadn't been worse, but young enough to be mystified by the idea that someone who had come so close to death could be thought of as lucky.

Reina wept for hours each day. The nurses finally asked if we could bring our own pillowcases because she soaked hers so quickly that the laundry room in the hospital was having trouble keeping up. Reina described the incident in painstaking detail to whoever would listen, whoever happened into her room, whether she knew the person or not. She explained how she had been turning the radio dial when she heard a shrieking sound, which she thought meant she was caught between stations. How there was heat and light—before there was anything else, there were those—and how something hit her thighs like a flick of someone's fingers. How it stung. And then how there was a shower of scraps popping across her lap. How she frantically tamped her legs as they were exploding into flames before her eyes. How she fell out of the car and she's not even sure whether she opened the car door herself or whether someone passing by opened it for her. How the street smelled like tar when she rolled on the ground. How her elbows stung from the gritty pavement. On and on. The nurses said that from their monitors, they could see her lips moving even at night, probably telling the whole story from the start, over and over again.

My father, my uncle, and I visited Reina the morning after her first night in the hospital. When we arrived, Reina claimed that the man in the bed next to hers taunted her all night, telling her repeatedly that she would never walk again. When my father, my uncle, and I peered down at him, he smiled to reveal a missing front tooth. He had casts on both his arms. My father looked back to Reina and, as he did with most everything, deferred the outcome to God.

"God will take care. Leave it in His hands."

He was not a traditionally religious man—no church on Sundays, no cross around his neck—but he had an uncompromising faith. This was not good enough for Reina.

"Look what His hands have done already!" she said.

Tito offered to get the doctor to set her straight.

"The doctors don't know anything," she replied.

"Why don't you just try to stand up?" I suggested, and everyone looked at me, first, like I was crazy and then, like I was a genius.

Tito clapped his hand on my shoulder. "I always knew you were a smart one, Ramón."

"Try it," my father said to Reina. "Stand up."

Then, "Stand up!" my father and my uncle started clamoring together.

The man in the bed next to her shouted, "*No se puede! No se puede!*" and laughed. It was a play on a popular soccer chant at the time, and it was meant to discourage.

Reina huffed and gingerly moved her legs to the side of the bed. Rings of gauze protected her wounds but she grimaced as her skin slid over the sheets. Finally, she had perched herself on the edge of the mattress. My father stretched his hand out to her but she refused it. She sat for a minute longer, her eyes wide, staring at the floor as if she believed it was waiting to swallow her whole.

"Come on!" Tito said, clapping his hands once, like cymbals.

"*No se puede!*" the man in the bed chanted.

Reina pursed her lips and then pushed off, like someone slipping from the edge of a pool into the water, and stood. She took a step forward as we watched.

"They feel very tight," she said, pointing to her thighs.

We all waited for more.

"But I can walk," she said defiantly, and then proceeded to do just that all the way to the bathroom in the corner of the room.

When she returned to her bed, the doctor, who had just come in, told her she needed to rest. Just because she could walk, didn't mean she should. At least not right away. Her body needed time to heal.

"God will make her new," my father promised.

"That would be very nice," Tito said. "A new woman would be very nice."

When my father shot Tito a glare, Tito raised his hands. "What, Francisco? I'm only joking!"

Reina said, "Why joke? A new woman *would* be nice. Then it wouldn't be *me* having to put up with you all the time." She raised her eyebrows at Tito.

My father laughed, though he tried to stifle it. "Come on, Ramón," he said, cupping his hand around the back of my neck and guiding me out of the room. "Let's leave the lovebirds alone."

My father, the story goes, entertained thoughts of priesthood until he met my mother. "Isn't that always the way?" he said to me once. "Who doesn't become a priest for any other reason? The Church has lost many a good man to the love of a good woman."

They were at a restaurant, a little *cabaña* on the causeway. They were both alone, at separate tables. My mother spilled rice water all over her skirt and my father saw her, he said, waiting for a server so that she could ask for a napkin. She sat very still, something he found curious since he assumed she must have been very uncomfortable. Finally, he went over to her himself and offered her a handkerchief, which she accepted and kept. My father returned immediately to his table without another word. Later that night, at home, with the hemstitched handkerchief washed and pressed, my mother noticed a small monogram embroidered in the corner. For the next week, she spent hours a day calling every listing under V in the telephone book and saying, "Hello, I'm looking for a man there who recently gave away his handkerchief." After hundreds of wrong numbers and hang-ups, she found him. She was lucky. My father wasn't even the one who answered the phone; his mother was. But he had told his mother that night when he came home from the *cabaña* about a young woman he had met briefly and how she had taken not only his handkerchief but also his heart.

Who knows why? Love between people is not something to be understood by onlookers. No one might have guessed that my father, a genial and charming man from the city, could have loved this whisper of a girl. But a transformation took place in him, and he saw something in her either that no one else could or that they refused to recognize. He saw a light, he would often say. Your mother is a light.

To almost everyone else, though, my mother was stark. A strong but quiet woman. My earliest memory of her is her slapping my back to expel water from my lungs after I nearly drowned in six centimeters of bath water she had run in the washbasin outside. I remember her face, frozen and dispassionate, no sounds issuing from her mouth—no screams, no prayers, no pleading—and the firm smack of her hand against my wet skin, the burning in my throat as the water shot forth.

Ubi, my best friend, doubts I could remember all that. The first time I told him, he explained: "You weren't even three yet, Ramón. It's been well documented that no human being is capable of remembering anything before the age of three." Ubi had discovered a volume on child development in the garbage dump along with some medical encyclopedias and, for fun, had actually been reading them. I saw him on his patio when I went over. Because of the stench left from the trash, he wore rubber gloves to turn the pages and a nose clip like the kind the leisure swimmers at the Intercontinental Miramar Hotel wore—nude-colored molded plastic pinching his nostrils together.

"I *remember*," I insisted. "Maybe I'm superhuman. The first person to have a memory before three years old. You should send a letter to those editors and tell them about me."

"They would never believe me," Ubi said, grinning.

"I swear. I remember," I said, and I did.

My Tía Reina had run out in her bathrobe when she heard me coughing. She snatched me from my mother and sat with me, locked in her bedroom, until my father came home that night. The whole thing sent a scare rippling through the house and deepened the sense of resentment toward my mother, whom no one in my father's family had liked very much from the beginning anyway. It was worse, I suppose, because I was the only child my parents ever bore. I never saw my mother as the woman who let me come so close to death, though. I saw her as the woman who had given me life twice in as many years. And for that, I have always known, I would give her all that I could.

NOVEMBER 12, 1989

My father was in the bathtub, humming "Popeye the Sailor Man." I could hear him through the door. That and "The Impossible Dream" were his favorite songs. "Popeye" was reserved exclusively for the bathroom; "The Impossible Dream" carried him everywhere else. He walked around the house and sang it loudly in a mock falsetto: *To dream the impossible dream, to fight the unbeatable foe,* his voice growing louder and more earnest the longer he went on, his fist pumping in the air. To him, Don Quixote's was the ultimate tale. A man on his horse charging into windmills wasn't foolish; he was brave. My father could hardly contain himself when he'd found out I had to read the whole novel in school last year. I wanted to skim through it. I was pretty sure I already knew most of the story anyway. But my father had other ideas. He wanted to sit on my bed with me at night and read it out loud. He wanted to act out the scenes with makeshift sets and household props, wearing a mesh strainer on his head as a helmet and straddling the arms of the couch as if they were his horse. He even called my mother Dulcinea for a while until she told him enough.

"Papi," I yelled through the door. "Lunch is ready."

"Spinach!" he cheered, and I could imagine him, filmy water to his chin, smiling at me.

"*Arroz con pollo* and *patacones,*" I told him.

He asked me to give him one minute. I went back to the kitchen and sat down.

"I forgot limes," my mother announced. She had an apron with small pink flowers tied around her waist. Her hair was pulled back, away from her face, though a few strands were matted down at her temples and in front of her ears. "Ramón, I need you to get limes."

My father had to have a lime in everything he drank

and Tabasco on everything he ate. Usually we had a bunch of limes for him, in a netted bag, somewhere in the kitchen. My mother would go so far as to cut them into wedges and put them in a plastic baggie in her pocketbook when we ate out, in case certain restaurants didn't have their own limes on hand.

"Mamá, no," I whined. I was trying to get through lunch as quickly as possible so that I could meet up with Ubi.

"Perhaps you know magic?" my mother said. "Maybe you could grow a lime tree here in the house and then we wouldn't have to buy them?"

I sighed.

"No? Okay, then. You'll go get some limes." She pointed toward the front door, like I was a puppy she was shooing along.

There was no arguing with her. Growing up, if there was something I wanted or some leeway I was begging for, it was better to go to my father. My father was strong in his own way and he could be very stubborn, but my mother was the person who, with one stern look, could prove that she was not to be tested.

She rooted through the change bowl on top of the refrigerator and handed me a few balboas. She held my shoulders with her hands and leaned to kiss me on the cheek.

"Stop," I told her, squirming away.

"You think you're such a man," she said, shaking her head. "Okay. You'll go to the Supermarket Rey and then come straight back."

I promised her I would.

The dogs next door barked from behind their fence as I walked by. "What do you know?" I asked them, and growled in return. I walked up our street—rows of houses with laundry strung out between them, pink paint peeling from the walls, red scalloped roofs—and stuffed the coins into my sneakers. We didn't live in a poor area, but we weren't exactly middle class, either. A few kilometers from here lived people who owned Mercedes with tinted windows and their own swimming pools. I had seen those houses, looked longingly through the gates at the ends of their driveways at the children jumping on big trampolines and playing T-ball on their sprawling lawns, but it was like watching a movie— something unreal and remote, some sort of fantasy I would never know.

We lived in the house that everyone in my father's family back to my great-grandparents had occupied. Strangely, not one of us had ever legitimately owned it. We had always rented it. The owners had changed over the years, but we—the Velasco family—had remained constant. It wasn't anything grand. There was only one room upstairs—an office filled with dusty suitcases and stacks of papers—and three bedrooms total: one for my parents, one for Reina and Tito, and one for me. The arched front door opened onto the living room, where a couch and matching loveseat were pushed against the walls and a small television rested atop an old metal vanity table. The kitchen was small, lined with wooden cabinets painted turquoise and crowded by a plastic-topped metal table in the center of it all. The only other space was a small laundry room—it used to be a maid's room but we used it for laundry—tucked off to the side of the hallway. Besides a washing machine, it housed a minirefrigerator where my mother kept bowls of Jell-O she ate when she wanted a snack, and a full-size ironing board that cut through the middle of the room. My mother's main effort at decorating had been to hang a cross, with palms from Palm Sunday tucked behind, in every room. Once, when I was in grade school and all my friends and I had decided that religion was stupid, I took the cross off my wall and threw it in the bottom of my hamper. When I came home from school that day, there was a band of crosses hung all at the same height around my room. My mother never said a word, but I knew it had been her. It was her way.

I wasn't wearing any socks and the coins were sticking to my feet. It was hot, though not more so than usual. The air was soupy and it smelled alternately of salt water and garbage. People sat on their patios and watched me walk past. A rooster pecked at a piece of concrete at the base of a bent section of fence that used to encircle a park here. Everything seemed fairly calm. I squinted against the sun as I made my way up the gravely road to where I would have to cross for the supermarket, about half a kilometer away.

Then I saw them: two lime trees in a neighbor's yard. They weren't more than ten meters from me. I snuck into the yard and over to the trees, though only a few of the limes on either one were ripe. I plucked the first four good ones I saw, waxy and dimpled, holding up the hem of my shirt to make a pouch to hold them. I had turned to leave when I heard a voice. I froze. I thought it was the owner of the house. But the voice was faint and it was clearly not directed at me. I took a step back and looked around. Across the street from the house was a laundromat, one my mother always said was too expensive, and behind that, an alley. There I could see, if I craned my neck, two men—about twenty years old, I guessed—standing beside a card table, arguing. It was difficult to hear what they said. I stood still and watched. One of the men—he had a rag slung over his shoulder—opened a trunk under the table and pulled out a handgun. He aimed it first at the other man and then turned and aimed it at various points along an imaginary arc. When he came to an angle where I thought he could see me, I ran. I dropped one lime, and the coins were pressing into my foot, but I ran all the way home, the fruit bouncing in my shirt.

This is what was going on: a certain lawlessness to everything. General Manuel Antonio Noriega Moreno, as I had seen him referred to in textbooks over the years, came to power in 1983 as commander of our armed forces. His popular nickname, because of his horrible, acne-scarred face, was *Cara de Piña*. My father said it was rude to call someone pineapple face, but I thought it was funny. No one really knew what to make of Noriega. Since the beginning of his rise to power there had been rumors about him: I'd heard that he'd planted the bomb that killed our former military leader, Omar Torrijos, causing his airplane to crash; that he was being paid off by the CIA in the United States to do their bidding; that he slept on a bed made from sacks of cocaine; that he smoked cigars with Fidel Castro; that he played cards with the shah of Iran. Last year, supposedly, he was fired by President Delvalle, but instead of leaving, Noriega had the National Assembly oust Delvalle. Then things started getting out of control. In March last year, the banks in Panama closed and the U.S. president, Ronald Reagan, forced all kinds of economic sanctions on our country. No money was moving in or out. Earlier this year, the U.S. troops started occupying the city in force, more and more of them all the time. People here went crazy. We all knew an invasion was coming. It seemed like an excuse to act up. Kids assembled homemade bombs and Molotov cocktails and tossed them at parked cars. People drove through the streets at night, hanging out their windows and honking at the U.S. tanks. Noriega was essentially handing out guns for free by this point, too, trying to build up a civilian army since everyone knew, if the United States really did invade, our own Panamanian Defense Force would have no fighting chance. I would have bet my life on the fact that those guys in the alley got their gun because of Noriega's directive.

I was panting by the time I got home. I waited for a few minutes on the patio, catching my breath before I went inside. I couldn't believe I had run. You would have thought I'd be used to the state of things by now. Not everyone was participating in the mayhem, though, not even most people. Just enough so that the city felt like it was skidding out of control. And just enough so that it was still surprising to see it actually happening before your eyes.

After a few more minutes of collecting myself—wiping the sweat from my brow, smoothing out the area where my shirt had been stretched from the weight of the limes—I finally walked inside.

"Ramón!" my father said. He clapped his tongue against the roof of his mouth and shrugged at me, his hands in the air.

"Your father can hardly speak because he hasn't been able to drink anything without his limes and his mouth is too dry," my mother explained.

"Very funny, Papi," I said. I placed the limes in a row on the table in front of him.

My mother cut one and poured him some water.

Then she said, almost in passing, "These aren't from the supermarket, Ramón."

"A vendor on the street," I told her. It was the first thing I could think of.

"Where?" she asked, and I knew it was a bad idea to keep up the lie because my mother's next move would be to drag me out to the street with her and have me show her the vendor.

But I said, "He was a traveling vendor. He had his limes in a wheelbarrow."

"And which direction was he headed?" my mother asked.

My father chuckled from his chair and I knew I might as well give up. I was about to apologize when my mother said, "This Sunday. You'll go to church with me."

I hated church. At the one my mother attended, they still said Mass in Latin, so I always sat there for an hour, not understanding anything. I hated the smell of the old wood and incense as soon as I walked in. I hated the women with their paper fans, fluttering them constantly. I hated seeing everyone afterward, standing around, talking, and no one ever talking to my mother, who didn't have a single friend that I knew of. She would smile at everyone and they would smile back and occasionally the priest would shake her hand, touch her elbow, and gaze warmly at her as priests do, and then she would shuffle me out and we would walk back home.

"But Papi doesn't go," I protested.

She looked at me with an unwavering gaze, though the corners of her mouth betrayed a tiny grin. "Papi doesn't steal limes, either," she said.

NOVEMBER 15, 1989

It was Tito's birthday. My father was buying a cake. Tito and Reina were both at work—Tito on the streets, holding bright orange flags to wave the cars around construction zones and Reina typing classifieds at a newspaper office. My father, a medical technician, had taken the afternoon off. My mother and I were in the kitchen. The radio was on, the light rumble of music fighting through the static. When my father walked in the house, he was balancing a huge white box with a cellophane top in his arms. I was sitting at the table, pulling the rinds off a pile of oranges.

"What kind did you get?" my mother wanted to know, without turning to face him. She was peeling

potatoes over the sink, thin ribbons of brown skin flying off and sticking to the sides of the basin.

"*Tres leches,*" he said, smiling proudly, as if he had
made it himself. He put the cake down on the table in
front of me. *Happy Birthday Tito* was scripted in bright
blue gel.

"Things seem quiet today," he said, walking toward
my mother. She didn't react. He slid his arms around
her waist from behind her. "Turn on the TV. You'll see.
They're talking about road construction."

"I would rather just listen," my mother said, turning
a potato in her hand, stripping it clean. "It's less of a
show."

Ever since talk of the invasion started, my mother
had sworn off the television. Even her *telenovelas.* She
didn't want the news breaking in, showing more images
that would terrify her. It had taken her a whole week to
even look at my aunt again after the bomb incident.
She had vigorously resisted going anywhere near the
hospital. When Reina was discharged and sent back to
the house, she was under instructions from the doctor
to stay in bed for at least another week. My mother
brought her chicken broth with rice for lunch and told
her what the lottery numbers were that day but aside
from that, she did her best to occupy herself in other
rooms of the house. Like a dog, Reina could sense my
mother's fear. On more than a few occasions, I heard

her asking my mother to change the gauze wraps because, she claimed, it was so exhausting to do it herself. Or, I heard her taunting, "Mariella, I'll just give you a peek." I conjured images of my aunt pulling back the sheet and raising the hem of her nightgown little by little as she said this. Often during that week my mother would emerge from Reina's room visibly flustered and hurry down the long hallway to another area of the house. There was something about actually seeing evidence of the destruction occurring throughout the city that was too painful for her to bear.

"How about you, Ramón?" my father said, ruffling my hair as I ducked out from under his hand. "You could probably go outside today."

I had already been outside with Ubi. We had poked at frogs all morning among the plants along the side of my house. Ubi had informed me that the Panama golden frog didn't have eardrums. He learned that in his encyclopedia.

"I don't feel like it," I told my father.

"Since when? It's a beautiful day for once. Go out. Enjoy. The party won't start for another two hours."

I shrugged. My nail punctured the fruit and sent a squirt of orange juice into the air. I looked at it angrily, as though it had embarrassed me when I was trying to appear cool. My father smiled and turned to pull a tin of soda crackers from the cabinet.

"I heard today that they shut down Café Esme," I announced. I saw my mother wince. "*Not* because of violence," I added quickly. She smiled at me gratefully.

"Why?" my father asked.

"To make room for something else, I guess."

"It's crazy," my mother said, leaning into the tile counter with her hip, "thinking of construction at a time like this."

"I appreciate it," my father said as he sat down at the table. "It's forward-thinking. Optimistic. This will be a better country soon. You wait."

No one said anything after that. It was as if we were waiting for it to change right then, before our eyes.

For the birthday dinner my mother prepared tamales, potato salad, a tray of *empanaditas*, and slices of pink pork garnished with orange wedges. My father's half sister, Flor, took a taxi from her apartment to join us, and some guys from Tito's construction crew came over as well. Everyone sat heavily on the couches and on the kitchen chairs placed around the living room. Two fans whirred from the corners but the heat that night was vicious. The fans were in a losing battle. The heat was like something you had to struggle through in order to move. It was easier to surrender and remain as still as possible. The front door and windows were open and what little breeze blew through, rustling the curtains, smelled of salt water from the bay. Far off, there were vague sounds—rocks tumbling, a car backfiring—the sounds of a city.

Everyone had a drink in his or her hand, the glasses wrapped in napkins to soak up the perspiration. My job was to walk through the living room and offer food to people. I made a few rounds, my mother handing me something new each time I re-entered the kitchen, but no one was really taking anything. Finally she told me just to wait for a while. She looked mildly dejected when she said it.

"It's just too hot," I told her, plopping myself down at the table.

"I guess so," she said, wiping a hand across her forehead and examining it. "I'm sweating a little."

In the living room, my father put on a cassette tape. It was his favorite musician, Cachao. Tito started telling a story—who knew what about—and suddenly they were all laughing. My father, whenever he laughed especially hard, made a flicking motion with his wrist that snapped his fingers against one another and created a loud pop. His face bloomed pink under his olive skin and he squeezed his eyes shut. I always loved seeing him like that. It seemed like something close to pure happiness.

My father called out to my mother and told her to join them.

Her gaze lingered on the food spread out on the table. "Try again with these in another minute," she told me before she walked to the other room.

It was the middle of November. In a month, I would be out of school for the summer break. Since the coup attempts had started back in October, I hadn't been to school much anyway. The schools weren't officially closed, but with everything that was going on my mother would rather me not make the trek there. The teachers and administrators seemed to understand. For a time, Ubi kept going every day but eventually he reported that they weren't really doing schoolwork anymore. Everyone was too distracted. Geometry and History had turned into opportunities for the teachers to open the class up to discussion about what was going on. The teachers liked to say that even though it hadn't been labeled as such, we were a country at war. They were trying, I suppose, to impress some gravity upon the students who still showed up. That so many desks were empty each day, though, seemed to me a more powerful indication of the seriousness of the situation.

Finally, Ubi stopped going to school, too, when there was no longer any point. We wandered to the outskirts of the city during the day because it seemed safer than downtown. Once, we took a bus out to where the *indios* lived and sat all day watching them piece together their *molas*. It was Ubi's idea. For research, he said. He had an intellectual curiosity that I have never, to this day, seen in anyone else. By the end of the day, two of the *indio* women invited Ubi back so that he could try making a small *mola* himself. We never returned, though, because both of our mothers—angry and worried—were waiting at my house when we got back to the city. It was close to dusk by then and they had been going out of their heads all day wondering where we could be, what could have happened to us. We tried to explain, but it didn't matter. It wasn't the time to be taking buses outside of the city. It wasn't the time to be doing much of anything, it seemed, except waiting to see what would happen next.

After a few minutes, I grabbed the tray of pork along with a box of toothpicks and walked around the room again. People took the food this time, piercing individual slices with a toothpick and sliding them onto a napkin. They thanked me as I moved to the next person. My Tía Flor pushed a dollar bill into my shirt pocket.

"Make it last," she whispered, and I nodded. I was used to this. Flor had never felt like part of the family so she was always the one complimenting my mother, giving me money, trying too hard. Years later, my mother would tell me that Flor was the result of an affair my father's father had with the wife of an American army officer stationed at the canal. It was a mess when the story surfaced. The army wife denied it until it was clear, from the appearance of the baby, that what her husband had accused her of was true. She handed Flor over almost immediately, telling my grandfather he was responsible for her. My grandfather, who didn't want to have to tell my grandmother about the affair, sent Flor to an orphanage. Over the following years, though, his conscience ate at him enough that he finally confessed everything. My grandmother, while not known as a forgiving person nor one to condone betrayal in any way, nonetheless insisted they raise Flor themselves. At least she was compassionate. And although they loved her the best they could, my mother told me, Flor never forgot the rejection in the beginning. Perhaps, my mother speculated, she was afraid of suffering that kind of rejection again.

I went back into the kitchen to start with the tamales. When I came out, my parents were dancing. It wasn't often that my father could convince my mother to dance but they were locked together, the hem of my mother's pale green dress swaying softly below her knees as she moved. My father had one hand pressed to the small of her back and the other held high in the air, clasping hers. They traveled the circles of the mambo with ease. One of the construction guys clapped in rhythm and everybody smiled.

"Hey, *mami*! We can't let them show us up!" Tito yelled over the music. "It's *my* birthday after all!" He pulled Reina off the couch. She made a little curtsy and patted her hair before stepping into his arms.

The construction guys were all clapping now and cheering them on. In the kitchen doorway I stood holding the tamales. Flor clutched her purse in her lap and smiled as she watched.

Amid all the music and the clapping and the excitement it was easy not to notice at first that someone had come to the front door. When Flor screamed, though, we all turned to look. I nearly dropped the *tamales*. All five construction guys stood up at once.

A small man with a thin mustache was standing in our living room, holding a briefcase at his side.

"My apologies!" he said, and took a step back.

My father stopped the tape and stepped in front of my mother.

"I only meant to get her attention," the man said, nodding toward Flor.

"He tapped my shoulder," Flor said, not taking her eyes off him.

"Who are you?" Tito demanded.

The man produced a business card from the inside pocket of his brown suit jacket and held it out, though no one stepped forward to take it.

"Ernesto Patillo," he said. "I'm here representing the Zoña Construction Company."

"We're not interested," Tito said.

Ernesto Patillo eyed my uncle wearily. There was an arrogance in his look, as though he had done this a million times before—barged into peoples' houses, had the same conversations—and in the end always got his way.

"I've been sent to make an offer," he said. "We've already spoken to the owner of the establishment and he has given his permission. As a courtesy, however, we would also like to extend our offer to you."

"What's going on?" Reina asked, looking worriedly at Tito. He put up his hand, signaling for her to wait a minute.

"We have plans to build a new apartment building here—"

Reina gasped. Ernesto Patillo glanced cursorily at her before continuing.

"And are prepared to offer you twenty thousand dollars to do so."

It was staggering. I had never heard a sum so high in connection with anything actually having to do with my own life. I had little concept, then, of the value of something like a house, and especially of something like a home. I thought we could move, somewhere better and more impressive, and we probably could have, but I didn't consider in that moment how much would have been lost.

Everyone was quiet, shocked into silence.

Finally, Ernesto Patillo cleared his throat. "As there is no decision, really, to be—"

"No," my father said. His voice was deep and clear.

"I'm sorry?" said Ernesto Patillo.

"No."

"As I said, we've already been in contact with the owner—"

"Of the *establishment*," my father said. "Yes, we heard you."

Ernesto Patillo cleared his throat. "Perhaps I'll send my manager over. I should let you know, however, that you'll need to vacate by the start of the new year. The construction will begin just after the holidays." He paused, again as if he was used to having this conversation, as if he was waiting to see if anyone would ask him why then, of all days. Confronted by silence, though, he offered an explanation himself. "It simply worked out that way in the schedule. As you can imagine, the company wanted to start as soon as possible but the crew was ready to strike unless we could assure them they wouldn't have to start work until January third. We're facing a very stringent deadline and unfortunately can't delay any more than that. I understand, of course, that this is terribly inconvenient but as the owner has already given his permission . . ." He trailed off and eyed us all with a look of mock apology, a shrug.

"You should leave," my father said. We were still frozen to the same spots we had been in when Ernesto Patillo first made his presence known.

"It's in your interest to take the money," Mr. Patillo said. He said it as if we needed convincing. I knew we would take it, though. We would be crazy not to.

"Okay," Tito said. "You've made your case. You have also, as it happens, interrupted our evening. It's in *your* interest to leave—now—so that we can get back to our dancing."

Tito turned the tape back on and pulled Reina toward him as we watched Ernesto Patillo leave. Flor got up and closed the door behind him.

I thought someone would stop the tape again in another minute, that the return to our revelry was only a show of defiance for Mr. Patillo. I thought they would have to stop so that we could absorb and discuss what had just happened. But Tito and Reina danced, my father and mother danced, and everyone else went back to watching. The mood was somber at first but after a few minutes and a new song, the hollering and laughing resumed, and everything was as if Ernesto Patillo had been nothing but a dream.

November 20, 1989

Since our mothers wouldn't let us go too far, Ubi and I started frequenting the neighborhood pool. We had discovered that we could sneak in through a flimsy piece of fence that lifted. We went in the mornings, stripped to our shorts, and tried to look our best for any girls who might be there. In the right light, it looked like I had a thin layer of hair on my upper lip, which I was sure gave me an edge over Ubi. We would dunk each other and do cannonballs when the girls weren't there but when they were, we sat rigidly by the side of the pool, our legs dangling in the water, trying to appear sophisticated as we discussed world events. We had memorized an exchange from a radio talk show that we would launch into whenever a girl we deemed worthy was within earshot.

"I think it would be fair to say we're in a state of crisis," Ubi would begin.

"But would it be accurate?" I would say.

Ubi would look very thoughtful and respond, "Consider the fact that President Bush has already botched at least one attempt. He's looking to redeem himself in the eyes of his people. The way to do that is to try again and this time, to get it right."

"I see. So the question is: What means will he use to succeed?"

Sometimes, we would get one of the lines wrong and we'd start laughing and forget the whole thing.

That day, during our third attempt at the conversation, a voice interrupted us.

"Don't you two ever talk about anything else?"

We looked up, surprised. Standing there, her hands on her hips, was a girl I had never seen before. She was not what I would consider one of the pretty girls. Her hair was short, and she was skinny as a straw.

"I was here yesterday and you were having the same exact conversation." She stared at us as if she expected an explanation.

Ubi appeared frightened.

"We feel it's an important topic," I said, puffing out my chest a little for effect.

"It is," she said, and I thought we were off the hook. "Important enough to use your own brains to think about it instead of regurgitating a debate from a radio talk show."

I felt myself blush. Ubi said, "Excuse me," and slid from the edge of the pool into the water.

"I'm still here," she said, when he came up.

She introduced herself as Sofia and sat down with us.

"Ramón," I mumbled.

"Ubaldo," Ubi said. It was one of the only times I had heard him refer to himself by his full name.

Sofia admitted she was impressed anyone else our age had listened to that radio show at all, much less taken the time to memorize part of it. I said something about how contemporary politics intrigued me. Ubi just nodded.

Sofia went to another school but was in the same grade as us. Her family had a membership to the pool, mostly so that her younger brother had a place to take swimming lessons. When she wasn't here, she was at her parents' seafood restaurant, seating people and clearing tables.

"There's my brother," she said, pointing to a dark, skinny boy held at the surface of the water by an instructor's hands on his belly. His arms were straight out, like Superman, and he kicked his legs furiously.

"I've never known anyone who couldn't swim," I said.

"You think it's a natural human instinct? You're just plopped into the water and you automatically start churning your arms and kicking your feet?"

I only meant that growing up near water, the ocean part of our everyday lives, it seemed like everyone figured it out sooner or later.

"Maybe," I said.

Ubi was on the other side of me, the farthest from Sofia he could manage.

"Oh, right," he said suddenly. "Like the time you almost drowned in six centimeters of water? Why didn't you swim then if it comes so naturally?"

I spun my head to him and narrowed my eyes.

"You almost drowned?" Sofia asked.

"He doesn't actually remember," said Ubi. "He's constructing what he thinks are firsthand memories from secondhand accounts."

Sofia seemed to understand this perfectly. "How old were you?" she asked.

I turned back to her. "Two and a half," I told her. "And I remember it like it was yesterday."

"Which explains why now you act like you're about three," Ubi said, laughing.

Sofia giggled too.

I clenched my jaw and watched the kids splashing in the pool, listened to them screaming.

Sofia leaned close enough that I could feel her breath against my ear and whispered, "Don't worry. People only float in salt water, anyway." I think it was supposed to make me feel better, and it did until she stood up and said, "Come on, Ubaldo. Let's get a soda," and I watched the two of them walk to the Coca-Cola stand at the edge of the pool.

NOVEMBER 24, 1989

My mother sent me to pick up the mail. The post office was within her circumscribed area that I was allowed to go while remaining, in her mind, relatively safe. In Panama at that time, people had post office boxes but no one, not even the wealthiest residents, had a mailbox at their house. If you were rich, you could send a messenger to get your mail, but there was no such thing as door-to-door service. We went once a week, usually, to pick up whatever correspondence had accumulated for us in the postal building near our side of town.

With each passing day, my mother was growing more averse to the idea of even going outside. She went to church on Sunday, dragging me along with her as punishment for stealing the limes, but beyond that, she remained in the house. She watched from the window as I hung the laundry in the backyard, making sure I was doing it right and yelling out instructions through the rusty screen if I wasn't. She put me in charge of picking up the coconuts after they had fallen from their tree and of trimming the banana leaves when they encroached upon our neighbor's yard. She made me take the curtains outside and beat the dust out of them with a paddle. She tuned the radio to a music-only station instead of one with newsbreaks, and she unplugged the television as if she was scared that without her even pushing a button, it might turn on by itself and deliver bad news. My father, for his part, had developed a more sullen aspect ever since Ernesto Patillo's visit. He tried to fight it, I could tell. But it seemed to overtake him at times and I would find him staring at a dark smudge on the wall or at a crack in the tile floor, completely absorbed.

"Look at this, Ramón," he said. "This is where the headboard on your grandparents' bed came to. It's a good marriage if there's a mark on the wall like this." He gave a small smile. "In imperfections, there's the evidence of life."

The post office was crowded, hordes of people in front of the huge grids of brass mailbox doors covering the walls. Just inside the entrance, a shirtless man slept on the floor, enjoying respite from the heat.

We received only two items that day: a water bill and a letter from the Zoña Construction Company. I tucked both under the waistband of my mesh soccer shorts and started home.

On the street, a man on crutches hobbled up to car windows, brandishing a bouquet of roses, pleading with drivers to buy just one. A boy younger than me pushed a sno-cone cart, the bell at the front making a hollow clank as the wheels bounced over pebbles. Stores were open. People bustled in and out of the air-conditioning, stopping to talk on the sidewalks and parking strips.

I was close to home when I heard the same voice from the other day—the guy from the alley.

"Hey," he said.

I kept walking.

"Come here."

I wasn't sure if he was talking to me but given the

fact that no one else was on the street, there was a good chance he was.

"I said come here!" he shouted.

I stopped—I don't know why—and looked at him. He had his shirt off. He was all bones and taut skin, his ribs like a grate over his chest. He wore dirty jeans with the same rag I had seen before threaded through one of the belt loops. A shorter guy stood beside him, a baseball cap on his head and an unlit cigarette in his mouth.

"Where are you going?" the first guy asked.

"Nowhere," I said.

"I've been there," he replied. I thought then that they were probably crazy. I don't know why I didn't just leave. We were still standing across the street from each other.

"I'm kind of in a hurry," I said.

"Don't worry. Nowhere will wait for you. It always does. I want you to see something."

"Come on," the shorter guy said, and motioned for me to cross the street.

I did, scared of what they would do if I didn't.

"How old are you?" the skinny guy asked.

"Fifteen," I said.

"A full-fledged man," his companion said. The cigarette bobbed as he spoke. The other guy laughed.

"Do you know what's happening, *joven?*"

I stared at them.

"Have you heard of the Dignity Battalions?"

Dignity Battalions was the name Noriega's paramilitary forces used, although I doubted these guys had anything to do with them. I nodded.

"Look, the Americans are coming. They have a shitload of equipment, you know. Tanks, bombers, machine guns. They think they're going to tear us up," the skinny guy said.

He paused and I nodded because I felt like I had to.

"We have to be ready. We can sell you something small for one hundred." He had lowered his voice now. "You want to see?"

I knew what they were talking about. "We already have a gun," I lied.

"You can never have too many," the shorter guy said.

I wanted to leave. The birds in the trees twittered like even they knew I was in over my head.

"Can I think about it?" I said.

"What's to think about? Come on. At that price? With everything that's going on?" He shook his head in mock disappointment, tsk-ing at me through his teeth. The corners of the letters were poking the inside of my thigh under my shorts.

"Please," I said. I didn't think they were going to give in.

Then the first man crossed his arms and shrugged. "Okay, you think about it, little man. You save up your money and come back to us. You're going to need it before you know it," he said and winked.

The other man pulled the cigarette from between his lips and tapped the end with his finger, watching me.

I nodded, backing away from them. I didn't run, I wouldn't let myself, but I walked as fast as I could back home, the gravel crunching under my shoes, my heart hammering in my chest.

Without a word, I handed the mail to my mother. She was standing in the kitchen. Not doing anything, just standing. I heard the samba music from her radio and thought, for the first time, that maybe my mother had the right idea.

DECEMBER 8, 1989

In the following weeks, we got two more letters from Zoña and each time my mother calmly tore it up and threw it away. Once, I pieced one together to see that it was an evacuation notice. That was what I had expected. I had no illusions about the compassion of the world; I knew the construction company wouldn't change their plans just because my parents didn't want to go. In the letter, there was a line, underneath a spot where the owner of our house had already signed, where my father was supposed to fill in his signature, but it had been left blank.

I asked at dinner one night, "When are we leaving?"

We were eating scrambled eggs with cubes of cheese and ham. Tito was having a beer.

My father stuffed a forkful of the eggs, like yellow clouds, into his mouth and said, "We are not leaving."

"I thought we had to," I said.

My mother cast her eyes down and didn't say a word. I looked to Reina and Tito. Reina was poking Tito and raising her eyebrows.

Tito swirled his beer in its amber bottle and said, "In ten days, Ramón. We're going to Cerro Viento. In San Miguelito." Tito let the rest of the beer run into his mouth and then swallowed it all at once. He shook his head as if he were trying to get water out of his ears. "Why don't you tell him, Francisco?" he said.

My father said, "We are not leaving."

"Eh," Tito said dismissively, waving his hand at my father. He turned to me. "Your Tía Flor found us a house there. She took it on herself—went around, looked at a few places, even got us a good price. Don't worry, you'll still have your own bedroom."

"It's a nice house," Reina said. "It has a huge patio in front."

"Everybody knew except me?"

"Someone *was* supposed to tell you, but I guess they forgot," Tito said, looking directly at my father. "Your aunt and I have already started packing."

"Are we taking the money?" I asked. It still sounded like a good deal to me: a new house, piles of money. I knew my parents would be sad to go, but they would readjust, they would see.

"You know, we *should* take the money!" Tito swayed slightly in his chair. His eyes were glazed. "It would be a shame to let it all go to waste."

"It's a bribe," my father said. He hadn't taken another bite in the last few minutes.

"It's a lot of money!" Tito said. "You could send Ramón to college or to the United States! It's a nice sum."

"Very nice," Reina consented.

I looked at my mother, who continued moving her fork mechanically to her lips.

"It's blood money," my father said.

"They're going to do it anyway, Francisco! Get your head out of the hole and try to understand what's going on here!"

My father's face, even under his dark skin, burned red. Then he looked at Tito and, of all things, smiled. "It's you who doesn't understand," he said.

Tito quieted after that and I didn't know what else to say. Soon I grew wrapped up in myself—thinking about what school I would go to over there and what the uniforms would look like, wondering how many buses I would have to take to get to Ubi's house, envisioning our new home and the neighborhood. Outside, the crickets squawked in their secret language and birds rustled in the trees. The muffled sound of cars honking filtered through the air amid the grind of machinery. Inside, we stayed silent and finished our meal.

DECEMBER 15, 1989

Ubi and I went back to the pool as often as we could. Sofia was almost always there, in her orange bathing suit. Ubi and I saved a chair for her if she wasn't around when we arrived, though Ubi would usually wander off and do laps in the roped-off area whenever she showed up. Apparently he wasn't interested in a girl like Sofia, which only made things easier for me. She brought a towel and newspapers with her and settled in by the water to read. I told her my aunt worked for *La Prensa* so I could probably get it for her for free, but she said she liked to pay, to support things she believed in. I had never thought of it that way.

Her face looked different to me now than when we first met. Her olive skin seemed almost translucent, like the skin of a fish, and her dark eyes were more playful, less hardened. I still thought she didn't eat enough—she lacked the hips that the beauty contestants on television had—but there was something gentle and effortless in how her body moved, and her slender neck, when she leaned forward to read the newspaper opened on her chair was, I began to believe, the most beautiful thing I had ever seen.

Often, Sofia and I raced backstroke across the length of the pool. At first, I would let her win, but when she caught on to what I was doing, she refused to play along. I viewed giving her a head start as a sign of deference, trying to be kind. She maintained it was the ultimate disrespect because it was like denying her ability. It was also egotistic, she said. As if I was so sure I would win, anyway. After that, I raced as hard as I could and won, but it afforded me an advantage all the same because when I reached the other end, I had time to stand and watch while she pulled herself into the concrete wall, her thin arms whirling, her hair swishing under the water.

At home, I lay on my bed at night and thought of her, often reaching my hand under my shorts and stroking myself until I shuddered, wetting the sheet. I had kissed two girls last year but neither had the lingering effect that Sofia had. Neither changed—nor had the capacity to change—the way I understood the world and myself.

When I told Ubi I thought I was in love, he looked crestfallen.

"What?" I said. "Aren't you supposed to be happy for me?"

He was quiet for a few seconds, as if he was considering carefully what to say next. "So are you going to spend all your time with her?" he asked.

I laughed. "No. Don't worry. She doesn't even know."

"I don't think you should tell her," he said. "She's not a typical girl. It might not be the kind of thing she wants to hear, you know?"

"Don't worry," I assured him. "We'll still hang out. I found the bus that will go to your house after we move. Nothing will really change."

Ubi had never been good at concealing when he didn't believe me, and his face betrayed it then. I felt nervous, too, not so much about Sofia, but about how moving to Cerro Viento would affect my friendship with Ubi. *Nothing will really change.* People say things all the time with the best of intentions but it's so easy not to believe the words that come out of your own mouth.

I thought a lot about what Ubi said, though, about Sofia not being the kind of girl who wants to hear professions of love. Truthfully, I had trouble even imagining what that scene would look like: what I would say to her, where we would be, what she would say back. In the end I settled on writing her a short postcard that would make my feelings known without being a whole overblown love letter.

I was upstairs sitting at the big green metal desk, trying to shake life into a pen that had dried up. The dust in that room was so thick I could poke my finger down into it like mud. Reams of paper were stacked all over the floor, some in manila envelopes, some bound by rubber bands. Pressed against one wall, next to an old bench, was my high chair from when I was little. I had my postcard—a glossy photograph of a girl in a *pollera*—in front of me. So far I had written *Querida Sofía*. I was rummaging through a rusty drawer for another pen when I heard Reina run in downstairs and shout, "It's happening soon! I heard it! They're coming." She scampered down the hall, calling my mother's name.

"Mariella," she sang, "you'll be so happy! Now you have a real reason to stay inside."

I hid my postcard under a stack of papers and crept downstairs just as my father and Tito, who gave my father a ride home every day, walked in.

Reina burst back into the living room, nearly breathless. "It was all over the newspaper office," she panted. "It even filtered down to us."

"What did you hear?" Tito asked. He laid his construction vest on the couch and walked to her.

Maybe she had been standing there for longer, but it was only then that I noticed my mother, in the shadows of the hallway, her eyes wide and unblinking. I couldn't tell whether it was fear or the horror of confirmation that made her seem so small, so weak. But when Reina started to talk again and Tito wanted to turn on the television, she said quietly, "You can watch the television at the *panadería*."

Reina frowned. "We have a television right here. You don't have to watch. Go lock yourself in the bathroom and we'll call you when we're done."

"It's my house," my mother said coolly.

Under her breath but loud enough for us all to hear, Reina said, "Not for long."

I expected my father to say something but I think he knew that this was a battle my mother wanted to wage on her own. My parents were always good at that—silent communication, sensing each other's needs by not much more than their pitch of voice, a tremble in the air.

"Leave," my mother said. "Go and watch your spectacle. That's what you want, isn't it? The excitement that comes with the threat? That's what gets you going. I thought you, of all people, would know better. But your legs? It was just another war story. Something to talk about and show off. Something to scare people. I don't want it in *my* house."

Reina and Tito both looked dumbfounded. My father looked proud. I had seen my mother hang up the telephone on people before or ignore beggars in the streets, but it was the first time I had seen her stand up to anyone like that and it would not be the last.

The four of us went to the bakery to watch the news. I think my father would rather have stayed behind, but again it was as if there were some unspoken code he was able to decipher. As if he understood that everyone leaving the house was the only way for my mother to feel like she had won. The bakery workers in their paper hats crowded behind the long pink counter, watching the small wall-mounted television along with us. The newscasters said that Panama had officially declared a state of war. Anything they reported next, I didn't hear. Despite the heat from the ovens pressing against my back, I remember feeling a chill run through me at the sound of those words. I remember feeling a quiet, creeping fear throughout my body, and I remember thinking about Sofia. Before that, every moment had felt like waiting. As though we were all, as a country, teetering on the edge of a cliff. We were peering down; we were holding our breath. We were on the brink of something, but we were waiting for some signal, some gust of wind to push us forward, to catapult us into action, into change. It came then. And we all, I think, wanted to believe that whether we jumped or fell, there would be something there to catch us, that things would be better once it was over.

DECEMBER 16, 1989

My mother was saying her rosaries when they arrived. I was upstairs, still struggling with my postcard to Sofia, when she called my name. I hurried downstairs.

A red housedress, scalloped around the edges with white thread, hung shapeless over her body. Her feet were bare.

"Ramón," she said, placing her hands on my shoulders and turning me toward the front door, which was open. "Go see who they are."

Who they were seemed obvious enough to me. Two construction men, in dirty khaki pants, white T-shirts, and hard hats, were walking around the perimeter of our yard, poking small orange and blue flags into the ground.

"Go see what they want," my mother said, giving me a little shove from behind.

I walked out and said hello. They presented me with work papers from Zoña and mentioned something about our mutual friend, Mr. Patillo. I told them he wasn't our friend but they hardly seemed to hear. They were scheduled to begin in a few weeks, they informed me, which I already knew. They seemed like nice enough guys. I told them I was sorry about them having to work right after the holidays. They shrugged and said it could be worse. I told them my mother and I were inside if they needed us, but they assured me that they just had a few marks to make—some bright orange spray paint and more flags—and they'd be on their way. Feeling very much like a man, one capable of taking care of his family and his property and matters of business, I shook hands with both of them before going back inside.

"What did they say?" my mother wanted to know.

"They're taking measurements. They won't be here long."

"We never signed anything," my mother said. I wasn't sure if she expected me to know what she was talking about.

"Have you seen the new house?" I asked, trying to shift her attention. Of course she hadn't, though. For the past two months, she had hardly left this one.

"I saw it in a dream," she said. "It was a mansion. And with so many windows." She had the detached look of someone absorbed in memories. "I was happy there."

Until then, I had assumed that my mother and father were of one mind in not wanting to leave our Velasco family home. But it seemed then as if maybe my mother wanted to leave, or at least wouldn't mind leaving. This house, after all, had turned into her prison—a prison she had built out of her own fears, but a prison nonetheless. My father, I realized then, was the one who wouldn't let go.

DECEMBER 17, 1989
For the past several days we had all been busy packing but my father insisted no one touch his things. He sat

in his favorite chair, reading my copy of *Don Quixote* at times, and retired to his room to nap at others. We continued to work around him, like water flowing around a boulder, taping boxes and balling our clothes into plastic bags. When the day came to depart, a small pickup truck sent by Tía Flor arrived mid-morning. It would take multiple trips to transport all our belongings. That morning my father had finally packed his personal items. I stood watching him as he pulled his *guayaberas* from their hangers and put them in suitcases and bags. He tapped the last hanger so that it sent a series of collisions shuddering down the row, the sound of the metal tinkling and echoing in the empty room. He dragged his fingertips over the grain of the wood on the closet door. He was solemn in his actions, but at peace.

"Papi," I said, startling him out of his contemplation. "Are you okay?"

"God will take care," he said.

Near the end of the day, when the furniture and boxes had been hauled away, we stood in the living room one last time. We threw out memories like letters into a fire, Reina starting by remembering the time— when she, my father, and Flor were little—that Flor came close to being stung by a scorpion.

"She was sitting on her bed, Francisco. Remember? Papá was standing in the doorway and he said, 'Flor, stand up very slowly and come here,' and she did. I was on the other bed because we had to share a bedroom." Reina looked at us like we should understand the imposition of having to share a bedroom with Flor. "And then Papá pointed to the wall behind her bed and there was this scorpion, its tail curled, only a few centimeters above where Flor's head had been. I jumped up from the bed, too, at the sight of that. Papá came back into the room with a pair of scissors and walked right up to it and held the scissors flat and snipped it in half. Both pieces—the head and the tail separately—fell onto her pillow. She made us move her bed after that, remember? She didn't want it there anymore." Reina laughed.

"I remember kissing you on that patio," Tito said. "You had on that white dress and, *mami*," he shook his head, "you were a hot thing that night."

"It wasn't long after that that white became, let's say, not *fitting* for me." Reina smiled teasingly at Tito.

"I remember bringing Ramón home from the hospital," my mother said.

"That almost didn't last long, either," Reina whispered, but we all ignored her.

"I took you around the house so you could get used to where you would be living. I said, Here is the bathroom, here is the television, here is the curio, this is a couch. I kept your bottles in the little refrigerator where I keep my Jell-O now." There were tears forming in her eyes as she said this.

It was my father's turn. He didn't say anything at first, though, so Reina spoke up again, providing a memory for him.

"Do you remember the time you knocked Tito's tooth out?" she said.

"What?" I asked.

She nodded. "Your father didn't like Tito at first."

"I have no idea why not," Tito said.

"What I remember is that Tito came to this house to pick me up for our first real date. We had met each other a few times before that. Just for sodas. It was innocent."

Tito snorted.

"I spent all day getting ready. I even went to the salon to get my hair blow-dried. That cost me two dollars then. It was almost all the money I had, but I thought it was worth it. Tito was supposed to pick me up at seven. He told me he was taking me to dinner. Francisco, remember? You and Mamá and Papá were sitting at the table, eating already, and I was stiff with nerves, waiting for my date by the door. Mamá didn't want to start eating, but Papá, who couldn't resist food in front of him, even for a second, said a quick prayer and was on his way. Then you all were. And I was still waiting." Reina raised her eyebrows pointedly at Tito. "I waited until nine o'clock. My makeup was a mess by then because I had been crying. Francisco, you tried to lift me out of the chair and carry me to my room. You weren't very strong, of course, so it did no good. Then, just after nine, I saw Tito strolling toward the front door, a toothpick in his mouth, like nothing was happening. Francisco saw him, too, and walked outside and slugged him, just like that"—Reina thrust her fist in the air—"and knocked him down."

"You did?" I asked, looking at my father.

"He did," Reina said. "You might not know this, Ramón, but your father can be crazy sometimes. If he gets an idea in his head, no matter how idiotic, he will do it. The only thing that wasn't like that was priesthood. And the problem with that was that he got an even more idiotic idea instead."

I must have appeared confused because my mother said, "She means me. She means he got the idea to marry me."

"Anyway," Reina continued. "Your father knocked out one of Tito's front teeth. He has a false one now."

"Really?" I asked.

Tito tapped a tooth with his nail. "This one right here."

"I'm telling you, your father can be very reckless."

"It's true," my mother said with a hint of admiration in her voice.

"Tell me more," I said.

And then finally my father chimed in. "I remember the time the electricity went out for a whole week. You remember, Reina?" She nodded. "There was not much to do besides eat and sleep. It was difficult to read at night by not more than candles. We couldn't turn on the radio. I was young. Restless, too, but Mamá wouldn't let us go out at night because the streetlamps and the traffic lights were off. I was so mad about having to stay inside that whole time. But that's when I fell in love with this house. It was like being blind. I experienced everything differently. The shock of the cool floor as I moved my feet over it was something I had never noticed to that degree. The rough feel of the walls as I trailed my fingers over them, trying to steer my way down the hall. I smelled the gas from the stove stronger than ever."

It seemed like he was going to say more but he stopped. I looked at him and saw my father, like my mother, on the verge of tears.

And me? I probably had the fewest memories of any of us, the least time to have accumulated them. But I felt my whole life swell in me as I stood there. *I remember everything*, I wanted to say. But instead I said, "I remember when there was furniture in here," and everybody laughed.

We squeezed into Tito's Datsun and headed for Cerro Viento. How strange it was that at the moment we had all come together, everything around us was about to fall apart. My mother kept her eyes closed for the duration of the ride, fingering the rosary in her lap.

Tito sang along to the radio as he drove and Reina tapped her nails to the beat against the dashboard. My father, a few last books piled at his feet, stared out the window. I watched it all go by: the gangly man selling dish towels to the cars stopped at red lights; the neon signs flickering as we passed an electronics store and the El Dorado mall; a car without wheels abandoned on the side of the road; billboards for new high-rises with picturesque scenes that didn't look anything like the plots they were being built on; a tank standing guard by a cinder-block wall painted with an Atlas beer advertisement; men in military garb lined up in front of corrugated metal doors that had been drawn to cover shops, whether with the owner's consent or not. I was paying attention to where the stores were in our new part of the city, watching the watery sun as it quivered low in the sky, and composing in my mind more of my letter to Sofia, buoyed by the novelty of love and the promise of change.

DECEMBER 18, 1989
The new house was a pale peach color. It was squat, only one floor, and looked smaller than our other house. But Reina was right about the patio; it was as big as a living room and just as welcoming. We could have parties here, I thought, and I imagined my parents dancing in the balmy night air.

"We're here," my father said, resting his hand on my mother's knee.

"Can I open my eyes?" she asked, and he told her yes.

She did so slowly, as if too much light too quickly would blind her, and then she smiled.

"It's nice," she said, but my father was already out of the car. "Do you think so?" she asked me.

"Sure," I said.

Next door a very attractive woman in a sundress and high heels was shaking out a rug over the railing of her patio.

"*Señorita!*" Tito called, and introduced himself as her new neighbor.

He was walking closer to the edge of our new property to talk further when Reina hit him on the back of the head with her purse. "Maybe Mariella can give you some tips on how to stay indoors from now on," Reina said.

Inside, the house was much newer than anything I was used to. Our old furniture, clumped in the center of every room, suddenly looked out of place. The kitchen cabinets had glass faces and the stove was white with six burners. The bedrooms were plain, with small windows covered by iron bars. The bathroom was tiny and lacking a tub. It wouldn't quite be the same to hear my father singing "Popeye the Sailor Man" in the shower. But it was clean and, as Tía Flor said when she came over later that night, it would just take some getting used to. As he entered each new room, my father looked more and more dismayed, like he had come with real—if resigned—hope, but now wanted nothing more than to turn and run back to our other house. I sat on the kitchen counter and watched everyone make their way through the rooms, walking in and walking back out, like visitors at a museum. I heard my mother say once, "Perhaps we can start a new Velasco history here." Absently, my father responded, "Perhaps."

I called Ubi when we had a phone hooked up. He sounded funny when he answered.

"What's wrong?" I asked.

"My mother's in the hospital."

"What happened?"

"It's called a pulmonary embolism. I looked it up in my book. It means there's a blood clot in her lung. I tried to call you but the number had been disconnected."

"We're at the new house now." He didn't say anything at first and I could imagine him nodding on the other end. "Is she okay?" I asked.

"I think so," he said. "She had surgery. Alma found her on the floor, passed out in the hall, and called an ambulance. When I came home, they were just putting her in."

"She already had surgery?"

"They had to do it quickly. The clot was blocking her lung artery."

"I'm sorry," I said. Alma was their maid, a short and stout woman who didn't talk much but who had been with the family since Ubi's father left, close to five years ago.

"She'll be okay," Ubi said. Then, "Are you scared?" he asked.

"Of what?"

"Everything that's going on?"

I thought about that for a minute. "I don't know. I want to see what's going to happen, I guess."

"Did you hear about those guys they got at Restaurante Campeon, over by El Dorado?"

"No."

"The owner was helping Noriega. He was holding a huge stash of weapons. The Americans stormed in and arrested him along with some of his employees. It's hard to believe. It was a popular place."

"That was one of Reina and Tito's favorite restaurants."

"At least you have your family," Ubi said. "It will be worse now, watching the news by myself, hearing about all that's happening. It would be nice to have someone."

Tito walked by me, sliding a box along the floor with his foot.

"You still have your mother. She's only in the hospital. She'll come back to you. And you have Alma. And you have me, you know?"

"Thanks," he said. "You promise?"

"Promise."

I gave him our new phone number in case he wanted to call. I told him I'd see him soon, anyway, though, and said that I'd have my mother say a special prayer for his mother because my mother knew all the special prayers for every occasion.

We lay our mattresses on the floor that night and, without sheets, went to bed in our new rooms. Even the insects here sounded different, their calls more shrill, and without anything hung on the walls to hide behind, the small lizards that I was used to seeing dart from picture to picture scampered along the seam where the walls met the ceiling, making their way around the perimeter like it was a racetrack.

I had trouble sleeping. At some point in the middle of the night I walked out to the patio. It was a flat expanse that was raised, level with the front door, and I sat at the edge with my feet dangling to the dirt beneath it. I held my postcard with the words *Querida Sofia* written at the top in my best handwriting. I sat for a long time, considering what I would say. Finally, I wrote, in small letters so everything would fit:

> I'm on the patio of my new house, across the city from where I used to live. It's different, though, like I have moved to another country. You told me one time that

you went to Costa Rica. What was it like? There are so many things I want to tell you. Like how I feel different when I'm around you. And how I wanted to kiss you the other day at the pool, after you rubbed chapstick on your lips. And how I think about you all the time and when I sleep, I dream about you. I wanted to tell you in person, but I wasn't sure how. I'm sorry for the postcard.

Ramón

I hoped it wasn't too much.

I was reading it over when I heard a shuffling behind me. I turned to see my father, in his white boxer shorts and T-shirt, walk onto the patio. Half of his dark, wavy hair stood straight up.

"What are you doing out here?" he whispered.

"I couldn't sleep." I slid the postcard under my leg.

"What do you have?"

"It's nothing," I said.

He sat next to me. I caught a faint whiff of his Aramis cologne as he lowered himself.

"It's poetry," my father guessed. I knew he was joking.

"No," I said. "It's a letter." I didn't know why I said it. I should have stopped at "No" and changed the subject, I realized.

"To a girl," he said and nodded.

I tried to deny it but he cut me off. "I sent a letter to

your mother once. I was in Chitré for *carnaval*. Her parents wouldn't let her go. I was having fun at first but I got tired of dancing with the other girls. The only one I really wanted was her. I had been thinking about her a lot before this. We had gone out a few times. But it wasn't until then—there was something that felt like it was missing from my life when she wasn't next to me—that I knew I had to be with her. So I wrote her a letter and told her."

"Did she write you back?"

He seemed not to hear me.

"Did she write back?" I asked again.

"She showed up at my door. Actually, I was outside already, hosing off our patio, and I saw her coming down the street on her bicycle."

"She rode a bicycle?"

"In a skirt, too. My mother always thought that was despicable, but I loved that about Mariella."

It felt strange to hear my father use my mother's first name, as if he had told this story before, to friends, and had forgotten to whom he was telling it now.

"What did she say when she saw you?"

"Nothing."

"Papi! Come on."

My father looked at me with his rough face, stubble that he would shave in the morning.

"She said, 'You've ruined me, Francisco. I won't ever

love anyone else.' We were both ruined by the other, I guess. People and things can do that to you."

He reached out and cupped his hand against the back of my head. We stared at the street for a few seconds.

"Ubi's mother is in the hospital," I said.

He looked at me. "What happened?"

"An embolism, I think he said."

"That's usually serious."

"Ubi said he thought she would be okay."

"Then I'm sure she will."

I looked up at the sky, at a perfectly round moon. It looked flat though. Less like a sphere hanging in the air than a hole that had been cut out of the blackness. And what if it was? What if it was a way to see through the sky to a layer behind it, one that was glowing and white?

Then, as if my father knew what I was thinking, he asked, "Do you believe in heaven?"

"Of course," I said.

"What do you think it's like?"

"I think there's a lot of light, even at night. And I think you can float a little, not like the astronauts in the space shuttle when they're bouncing off walls, but more like when you're in the ocean and you can spring up and hover for a second before coming back down. I think you can see down to earth whenever you want and that God's arms keep growing longer and longer every day because He wraps them all the way around heaven and holds everyone at once."

My father pulled me toward him and pressed his lips to my temple. He held them there, smoothing his other hand over my hair, like I was a child who had been lost and now found. He wouldn't usually do something like that but I knew he was feeling emotional about the move. I think he felt like he let go of his family by leaving that house. And if he wanted to hold on to me because I was still here and because he could, then I would let him. After a few minutes, he pulled away.

"It's time to get some sleep, Ramón," he said.

I followed him back inside and tried again to go to bed.

DECEMBER 19, 1989
In the morning, our house was the scene of an unpacking frenzy. I stuffed some clothes into my dresser drawers and then pulled on my soccer shorts and a T-shirt with a picture of a dancing dog on the front. I still had the money from the limes. I had kept it with me all this time, thinking that my mother would eventually ask for it back but she never did. I slid the coins in my shoe. My postcard to Sofia was on the floor next to my

mattress. I picked it up, careful not to glance at anything I had written. I didn't want to read it again. I wanted to trust it, to send it out and see what would happen even as I hoped that what would happen would be that Sofia wrote me back or called me or pulled me aside at the pool to tell me she felt the same.

I snuck out of the house amid the shriek of tape ripping off boxes and the sound of packing paper being unwound and uncrumpled and pushed aside. If I had told my mother I was going out, she never would have let me. For days now, the newscasters had come on television and told everyone to stock up on groceries and water because the invasion was imminent. Reina went out once and bought a few things and then nothing happened. On the streets people were trying to act as though nothing unusual was going on. They were still trying to conduct the business of everyday life, moving around sandbags and stacks of tires, ignoring the fact that so many stores were closed. And yet, there was an unease that had settled over the city like a filmy layer of dust. The streets were no more dangerous than they had been for the past two months, yet the promise of more danger was palpable. We were still teetering, it seemed. We were *so close* to falling.

At the post office, I fished the money from my shoe and used it to buy a postcard stamp. The man behind the counter gave me a phone book to look up Sofia's address. He acted very exasperated at having to do so. Carefully, I wrote Sofia's name and street in the space on the right side of the postcard and, with a great summoning of fortitude, handed it to the man.

He looked at the address and then looked at me.

"It's going to come right back here," he said.

"I know."

"Then you didn't need a stamp, *joven*. I could have put it directly in the box."

"So?" I was anxious enough as it was without learning that I could have saved my money.

He smirked. "Must be an important postcard." He flipped it to the back.

I flung my hand over it and pinned it to the counter. "Don't read it."

"I knew a Sofia once," he said.

"Please, just send it."

Someone behind me in line coughed.

The man at the counter looked up. "Whatever you say, *joven*." He shrugged and slid the postcard into a slot.

I wandered around for a long time after that. At first because I was annoyed with the man at the post office and then because I was all wound up with nervousness, restlessness, eagerness over the postcard. I didn't know where I was going. I watched the pavement pass under my feet and grew lost in my thoughts. More than once,

I had the urge to run back to the post office and beg the man to find the postcard and pull it out and save me. After a time, the squawk of a huddle of chickens jolted me and when I looked up I saw, about half a block away, the pool. It meant I had walked nearly four kilometers. Sofia was probably there, I thought, though I didn't feel in the best state to see her. Just knowing that my feelings were out there in the world, on a piece of paper, on their way to her, was almost the same as if she already knew. I felt that if I went to the pool she would be able to see right through me, that she would somehow be able to read on my face all the things I had written. But in another way, I longed to see her. I could tell her about our new house and even invite her over. Maybe she would have been in the water just before I arrived and her hair would be wet and pushed back from her face. She cut it herself, she told me once, not for lack of money, but because she couldn't stand all the primping and preening that went on with Latin American women, always at the beauty parlor, getting their hair bleached until it came out orange when really they wanted to be blond, getting their nails done, having fake eyelashes stuck on. My mother never does any of those things, I had told her.

"She's one of the enlightened ones," Sofia had said.

Or probably she would be reading the newspaper,

sitting up with her legs in a pretzel, gazing down at the opened paper.

"People who lie on their backs, holding their books up, are not reading," she had informed me. "It's impossible. Too much sun. They just want to *seem* like they're reading. I hate that."

I smiled now thinking of her saying such things. I had never known anyone so sure of everything she did.

I kept walking but by the time I got to the pool, I still wasn't sure whether I would actually go in. Maybe I would just peek in for a minute, to see if she was even there, to watch her for a second if she was. I stood outside the fence, my fingers laced through its metal diamond pattern, and watched the water rippling within its concrete bounds. People sat on towels and chairs, smoking or sleeping. The guy behind the snack stand was delicately building a tepee out of straws. And then I saw them—Sofia and Ubi. Her dark hair was wet, just like I had thought, but she sat in the corner, on the concrete, where two walls of the fence met, and Ubi sat beside her. They both had their legs crossed but they were close enough that their knees touched, and they were talking in a way that seemed undeniably private.

I knew it then.

I knew, watching them interact, that there was something between them. It was plain. And when, a few seconds later, Sofia reached out and held Ubi's hand, I stayed and watched, somehow unable to move, as if my feet had sunk into sand up to my ankles at the beach when the waves run back out. I stood helplessly, aware of the blood gushing through my veins, and watched them. Finally, when the attendant and the lifeguards weren't looking, I pulled back the flap in the fence and climbed through. My heart felt huge in my chest, like it was eating everything else inside me. Ubi saw me first and jerked his hand out of Sofia's. He stood up.

"I can't believe you," I whispered when I reached him. Sofia stood, too.

"I was telling her about my mother," Ubi said.

And for a second I wanted to believe that I was wrong, that the affection I had seen between them was only compassion and genuine friendship.

But then Sofia said, "His mother wants to meet me. She can't believe her son actually has a girlfriend." She smiled. How innocent she was to have said it. Of course she didn't know anything about how I felt. To her we were all friends and going out with Ubi was nothing— not a betrayal, not heartbreak.

I stared at her. I thought of the postcard she would receive in a few days. I wanted, for the first time in years, to cry, a heat burning behind my eyes.

"Ramón," Ubi said imploringly, reaching out to touch my arm.

But I pulled away.

"I have an errand," I said, barely able to talk without my voice breaking. I could feel the flood rising in me. I walked quickly to the other end of the pool and ducked back through the flap in the fence. I trudged home in a daze, my body heavy as lead, my eyes swollen and wet, and thought of what a fool I'd been.

DECEMBER 20, 1989

Early in the morning, when it was still dark, a loud boom shook the house and woke us. From the patio, where I had been the night before, everything looked different. Flares flew overhead, like firecrackers that wouldn't burst, and every so often, through the dark, a bluish explosion would illuminate a whole section of the sky. Except for my mother, we were all standing outside. My mother had taken her pillow into the shower stall and chosen to stay there. With all the tile, she said, it was the most fortified part of the house.

Beyond knowing that, finally, the invasion had started, it was hard to tell what was happening.

"It's all coming down on El Chorillo," Reina said after a while, signaling to where the red haze of so many fires could be seen in the distance. El Chorillo was an old neighborhood filled with wood-frame buildings that had been built at the beginning of the century. I wondered why they had started there. Maybe they were taking the neighborhoods one by one. Maybe ours would be next.

Lights popped on inside houses up and down the block. Our neighbors started appearing on their patios. Everyone was asking what was going on and no one had the answer. From two doors down a man in an untied bathrobe came around and told everyone that he had been listening to the government radio station and that they had advised everyone to stay in their houses.

"Then why are you out?" Tito yelled, but the man just shrugged.

My father went inside to call Flor. Miraculously, the phone lines were still working. But what she reported was worse than what we were experiencing. People were prowling around, breaking into cars, knocking on doors and threatening to come in for "inspections." In the midst of the commotion, every troublemaker had been loosed, feeling they had the right to terrorize anyone. On Flor's block, the neighbors had set up a patrol with a few of the men gathering weapons—machetes, bats, pipes—and standing guard so that everyone else could go back in their houses without worrying that anyone would break in. One of the men was equipped with a megaphone and was supposed to shout if there was trouble they couldn't contain. Flor sounded scared, my father told us. She hardly had any toilet paper or any groceries, either, and no one knew when it would be safe enough to go out again or when the stores would be open. My father instructed her to barricade her doors with furniture and to stay clear of windows. He promised, as long as the phone lines were working, to call her every hour.

After standing on the patio for a while, hearing the same explosions in the distance over and over, it became clear that our house wasn't in immediate danger. Occasionally, a helicopter or jet flew overhead and the sound of machine-gun fire erupted. I wanted to know what was happening everywhere else, but even after my mother was asleep in the shower and I turned on the television, there was only a fixed screen with a picture of the United States Department of Defense seal on it. I thought about Ubi at his house, his mother at the hospital, Sofia in her room, the worker at the post office, our old house, my school, the Intercontinental Miramar Hotel, my favorite pizza restaurant, Napoli. Sometimes I imagined it all destroyed, crumbled, people buried in the rubble. And sometimes I saw it all standing strong, the fighting something that was happening in our city but somehow much farther away, or at least more contained, enough so that it wouldn't touch us.

There was no rest that night. I would doze off for a few seconds before being startled awake again by another boom or by fear. All through the night, because

I couldn't stay still, I saw Reina and Tito and my father wordlessly wandering around the house. We felt compelled to stay alert in case something happened. We bumped into each other, we peered out the windows, and only my mother woke the next morning rested.

The looting began as soon as it was light. Everyone was taking advantage. People were walking down our street carrying mattresses and office furniture and plastic bags filled with clothes. Our neighbor from across the street told us a story about a man who had gone to an apparel factory and taken hundreds of socks. They were beautiful fine-stitched navy blue trouser socks. The problem, though, was that when the man got home and dumped them on the bed to show his wife, he realized he had taken only the left sock for each pair. The lefties and the righties were probably separated into different bins but he didn't know. Our neighbor laughed immodestly when she told us this story, slapping her thigh and showing all her teeth. She told the same story all day to anyone passing by and all day I heard her full and billowing laughter, a sound discordant with the blast of machine guns and the clamor of people looting only blocks away.

My father continued to call Flor every hour. She said that she had seen three Dignity Battalions steal a car in front of her house and that she'd heard at least two women on her block had been raped. "Where is the military?" she kept asking. She was hysterical crying. At midday, she reported that things were calming slightly and that she was going to have condensed milk and rice for lunch. I heard my father tell Reina that Flor had asked him if he thought her father had anything to do with this. I knew Flor was adopted but I didn't know the full story then. The question only made sense to me much later.

The sound of gunfire was sporadic during the day and increasingly, huge bomber airplanes, sending a heavy, dragging noise reverberating through the air, flew over us. No one went to work. We all stayed near the house, stepping onto the patio sometimes, and flipping through the static on the radio, trying to glean any new information. We kept hearing the same thing: Stay indoors, don't go near windows, stay tuned. I felt like an animal in a cage: My space was big enough for me to walk around, but I was restless and I kept coming back to the same spots—the front windows, the patio—to see if there was anything new. There wasn't. It was always the same faces out on the street, always the same small explosions in the distance. Ubi called in the afternoon, but I didn't want to talk to him.

My father had answered the phone. When he hung up, he looked at me sternly and said, "Now is not the time, Ramón."

"For what?"

"To deny your friends."

I shrugged him off but in truth I felt conflicted. I knew he was right but if it had been any other day, I would have felt justified in my anger toward Ubi. He had stolen the first girl I loved.

Ubi and I had been friends since primary school. We were paired together on a science project, dissecting worms. Ubi and his mother had just moved to the city after Ubi's father left them. Almost all the boys in the class were eager about the dissections—we had all been talking about it for a week—but when it came time to do it, I watched Ubi slice down the length of the worm's body with a steady hand and, totally unflustered, scrape out the different organs one by one, according to our work sheet. All the other boys were goofing around, poking at the worms, rolling them back and forth from one partner to the other. Our teacher was still talking about the first incision when Ubi raised his hand to announce we were done. It wasn't so much that he impressed me: At first I kept asking to be his partner because he did all the work for me. We talked, though, too, and over time we became real friends, eating together at lunch, riding go-carts on the weekends, getting into trouble. I couldn't remember a time, ever, when I'd been angry with him. Not until now.

Later in the evening, I considered calling him back,

but after lingering by the phone for a few seconds, I climbed into bed instead, hoping to find some rest.

DECEMBER 21, 1989

My father went to work. My mother pleaded with him not to leave, but he told her he had to.

"All that gunfire is hitting someone out there," he said.

I didn't want him to go either. "What if it hits you?" I asked.

"There's always heaven," he replied. "You told me what it would be like."

The color drained from my mother's face and she hit my father's shoulder. "Don't say that, Francisco!"

My father took her face in his hands and pulled her to him, kissing her right on the mouth in a way I wasn't sure my mother had been kissed in years.

"I'll be okay," he whispered, their noses touching. Then he left. He had to walk the three kilometers to work because none of the buses or taxis were running. I watched him start out on our street, zigzagging through the people scurrying with more stolen goods—today, apparently, a hat factory had been raided, along with a supermarket, metal carts and all. My mother went back into the shower stall and closed the door, emerging from the bathroom for brief moments, only when the rest of us needed to get in, waiting for ten hours until he came home.

That night, we sat at the kitchen table, my father telling us what he had seen. Reina munched on pork rinds since there was little else in the house for dinner. I hadn't eaten much of anything in two days, but I hadn't thought much of eating either.

My father said he had had to duck a few times to avoid sniper fire from various apartment buildings. "People don't even know what they're shooting at," he said. "Everyone has lost their mind."

The hospital where he worked was a disaster. Because there was no public transportation running, people had been calling for ambulances when all they really wanted was a ride somewhere. The result was a shortage of ambulances for those who actually needed them. Relatives and friends were walking in carrying their loved ones, many of whom died by the time they got there because the trip had taken so long. He told us about one woman who had walked in with her husband in a wheelbarrow. He had been standing guard outside his corner store and a van had rolled by, the barrel of a shotgun sticking out the window, and he had been shot twice in the legs. Reina instinctively touched her hands to her thighs and winced. My mother, as usual, was quiet.

"Did you hear anything," Tito asked, "about what's

going on? Are they close to getting him? You know, things like that."

My father shook his head. "It's too hard to tell. Everyone says something different. Maybe I'll find out more tomorrow."

I saw my mother cast her eyes up toward my father, questioning him.

"I have to go back," he said to her. "There was hardly enough help as it was."

My mother kept staring.

"Mariella, they need someone."

I could tell it was difficult for my mother to argue. My father had always had a noble and generous spirit. I imagined that was one of the reasons she married him. It made sense that my mother was scared, but in the end, as she always would, she trusted my father to the core of her bones and let him do the things he needed to without standing in his way.

"I asked around about Ubi's mother," my father said, looking at me. "She had surgery, but it went well. The doctors weren't sure whether to go through with it because she was scheduled for the day when everything started happening around here. They were afraid the electricity would go out in the middle of it. But I heard she was very weak so they went ahead early. She'll probably be released soon."

I had forgotten entirely about Ubi's mother being in the hospital and a surge of guilt pushed through me. I felt ashamed then at not having called him back yesterday. I could tell my father wanted me to feel that way.

I phoned Ubi's mother the next morning. The first thing she asked me, of all things, was if *I* was okay. I told her I was and that we were all thinking about her, my mother doing special prayers. I heard voices in the background.

"Ubaldo's here. You want to talk to him?"

But I heard Sofia, too. I knew it was her. I could imagine them sitting side by side in his mother's white box of a room, entertaining her and laughing. I could imagine Sofia with her thin fingers turning down the blanket, trying to be helpful. I didn't know what she'd be wearing, since I'd only ever seen her in a swimsuit, but I saw her face perfectly, her clear olive skin and a smile that exposed one of her incisors overlapping the tooth next to it.

"That's okay," I said finally. "You should spend time with him. I can talk to him later."

I didn't know whether she was aware that Ubi and I hadn't talked for almost a week now. But if she was, she didn't let on. She simply thanked me for calling and told me to tell my mother that she appreciated the prayers. I promised I would pass along the message and hung up.

December 24, 1989

I had lost ten pounds. A neighbor brought over a plastic bag full of stale rolls, offering us a few. I ate them happily. The cafeteria at the hospital had been closed for days, and people had already raided the refrigerators and storage closets, but my father managed to bring home some packets of sugar and ketchup and mayonnaise that he laid on the counter for us. We got creative. We mixed coconut juice from the coconut tree in our front yard with sugar and ice. We crumbled our last sleeve of Maria cookies onto a piece of browned lettuce and sprinkled it with beads of sticky rice and flakes of red pepper. We combined beans, Tabasco, and water until it formed some kind of stew. Reina and I performed a mock cooking show to pass the time, speaking in the affected voices of cooking show hosts and indiscriminately combining ingredients to see what we could come up with next.

The government radio station had been struck and our small black radio offered nothing but a steady buzz. I kept thinking about Sofia and about Ubi, wondering if they were okay. From what I could see, they probably were. The smoke and thunderous booms were concentrated mostly in one area, far from Ubi's house. Every day I thought about calling Ubi but something always stopped me. It was an immature idea, I suppose, that if I didn't talk to him for long enough, he would come to understand how upset I was and, knowing that, would have no choice but to stop being with Sofia. If he was a real friend, I kept thinking, he would understand. Even then, I didn't want to admit what I probably knew, which was that Ubi was better for Sofia than I was. My young ego focused on the fact that my voice was deeper than Ubi's and that, therefore, that I was more desirable, that Ubi had never even kissed a girl before so he would make a terrible boyfriend. I just walked around the house feeling alternately sorry for myself because of having my heart broken, mad because of being betrayed by my best friend, grateful because in all the chaos Sofia's postcard wouldn't be delivered for a long time, and anxious because after the invasion was finally over she would learn how I felt.

My mother desperately wanted to go to Christmas Eve Mass. She had been talking about it all day. There was a church just down the street from the entrance to our neighborhood, she said. In the morning, Reina declared she was not going anywhere.

"We can have Mass here," she said defiantly.

"Look who won't leave the house now," Tito taunted her.

"This is a different situation! People are getting killed out there." She waved her hands around in the air.

Tito shook his head. "No, *mami.* Same situation, different stage."

"You haven't been outside much either," Reina said.

Tito laid a hand to his oiled hair. "But I'll go tonight. No problem."

Reina crossed her arms and muttered a hrmph.

In the end, we all went. Even Flor met us there. The Mass was at five o'clock and when it was time to leave, my mother—dressed in a gold suit jacket and black skirt, her dark hair washed and loose, curling around her face—led us out the door as if she had been going for walks every day on these streets and today was just one more. Outside, the smell of smoke wafted through the air and stung my nostrils. Along the pavement, papers were strewn everywhere, bunched up near gutters and matted down. We passed two dead dogs, still in the middle of the road. I don't know why, but I expected to see Christmas decorations, lights and plastic pictures of Jesus up in people's windows. Even though we hadn't done anything about Christmas, I somehow thought that other people would have. Maybe I thought that if I got far enough from our house, I would find the Panama I had always known. But what I saw all the way to the church was the same as what I had been seeing from my one vantage point for days—gray sidewalks; over-tall grass and weeds; bits of trash everywhere; everyone on their patios, staring out at the street with absent owl eyes. The invasion had given us the veneer of sameness. We were one people going through hell.

The church echoed when we walked in. In the front, a pianist tapped the first few notes of each song he would play that evening. The church was a cavern, much larger and darker than our old church. A wooden balcony ran around our heads, occupied by two standing fans. Yellowed glass pendant lamps hung from heavy iron chains, casting dim light over the long dark pews. We all shuffled in, dipping our fingers into what holy water hadn't evaporated, and slid into a pew near the front. Besides the pianist and us, only one couple and an older woman were there. My mother knelt and prayed, keeping her eyes on the crucifix that hung behind the altar and pressing her rosary to her lips. She seemed in command here, in her element, while the rest of us sat uncomfortably in the pew—Reina taking quick looks over her shoulder at the open doors; Tito flipping through the missal, making an awful crinkling noise with the tissue-thin pages; my father staring solemnly at his hands; Flor writing out a check for the church to leave during the collection; and me running my fingernail along the grooves in the pew where the wood had weathered and cracked.

Another older woman came in just before the Mass started. She walked up to the woman already seated and poked her with her cane.

"What are you doing here?" she asked. She was practically shouting and her frail voice bounced off the walls of the church.

"It's Christmas Eve," the woman replied, shouting back, and I realized that neither of them could hear very well.

"It's too dangerous for an old woman like you," the woman with the cane said and laughed. She was missing almost all her teeth, and her gums, brown and purple like a bruised plum, flashed for an instant.

"Ah." The other woman waved her hand. "I wasn't even supposed to live this long. If they're going to get me, let them come get me."

Her friend nodded and sat down next to her.

Flor started crying. "A woman in my building died of a heart attack from the shock of the invasion," she told my father through sobs. He put his arm around her shoulder.

Reina looked at her, disgusted. "So delicate," she said. "Your name suits you."

"And who was the one I almost had to carry out of the house because she was afraid to go outside?" Tito asked her.

"*Oye*, I walked out on my own two feet!"

Tito grinned. "And it's a good thing, too, *mami*, because I'm a strong man but I might not have been able to carry you."

I laughed under my breath. My father looked at both of us, scolding us with his eyes. My mother, undisturbed, ignored us all and continued her prayers.

When the priest came out, he didn't walk up the aisle to the altar. He simply emerged from the sacristy while the pianist played "O Holy Night" until the priest put up his hand for him to stop. We went through the Mass like normal. The night seemed quieter than it had in days. Before the homily, the priest paced back and forth in front of the altar. He introduced himself as Father Castillo and thanked us for coming. Then he paced a bit more and said, "We have endured days of great stress. I know, for most of you, it was a trial simply to be able to come here, to come to church to observe our Lord. How wonderful it is to be able to hope that perhaps by next week, there will be no obstacles standing in your path. How wonderful to dream that soon this misery will be over. With General Noriega turning himself in to the Vatican Embassy today, there can be little doubt that the Lord our Savior is indeed watching over us."

The priest paused and looked up, clasping his hands. I turned to my father.

"What happened?" I whispered.

But my father looked as confused and surprised as the rest of my family did. No one else in the church had even flinched.

The priest had started again, about Mary and Joseph and their travels to the manger, but I needed to find out. I raised my hand. My mother looked at me and grabbed my wrist, pulling my arm down. I raised my other hand. She leaned across me to get hold of that one, too, but I wiggled it higher.

The priest furrowed his brow at us. He stopped in mid-sentence. "Yes?"

I stood up. "Noriega turned himself in?" I asked.

"Earlier today. He's seeking refuge in the Vatican Embassy."

"Does that mean it's over?" I could feel everyone staring at me. I gripped the top of the pew in front of me.

"Not yet. But God willing, it will be soon."

My mother yanked me down from behind, tugging on my shirt.

"Didn't you want to know?" I asked her as I fell back into the pew.

"You've interrupted Mass, Ramón," she said. But I could tell: relief and hope flickered in all their faces.

After Mass, my father wanted to stay and go to confession.

"What do you have to confess, Francisco?" Flor asked.

"I need to go," he said.

He looked uneasy walking into the confessional and

my mother said to me, "You see, Ramón. That's how you get when you don't go to church as often as you should." She laughed—I swear the first time I had heard her laugh in weeks—and my heart soared at the sound of it. All of a sudden I felt as if everything in the world was going to be okay. Hearing her laughter cut through the gaping space of that church, I thought it was the end of grief in our lives.

JANUARY 3, 1990

Over the next week, things continued to calm. In the beginning, it seemed we were never able to relax completely. Every time we stopped thinking about the invasion for half a second, something happened to put us on edge again. But now that Noriega had holed himself up in one place, there was only the matter of getting him to come out. The embassy was sovereign territory. Soldiers weren't allowed to simply storm it.

The television was broadcasting again and my mother, after our outing to church, had shed her old fears, letting them slide off her body like snakeskin. She no longer took refuge in the shower stall, no longer knelt on the couch while watching out the windows, and no longer put up a fight every time we wanted to turn on the TV. By contrast, my father grew increasingly somber. It was like the two of them had seeped into each other, displacing what used to be theirs with qualities from the other person. My father went to work and when he came home, he went to the bedroom. I would walk by the doorway and watch him through the long opening. He was back to reading *Don Quixote*, but he read it with tears welling along the rims of his eyes now, like a brimming trough ready to overflow. I hadn't heard him sing "The Impossible Dream" in what felt like ages. There was also a photograph, a small, square browned one, of his parents standing in front of our old house, that he would hold in his hands while sitting on the edge of the bed, hunched over, fingering the soft corners absently as he gazed at it. He was in mourning, my mother said. First, there was denial and then, with everything that was going on, he had hardly had time to think about the fact that we had moved. But now it had crept up on him and, as if he had lost a loved one, he would need time to pull himself back together. My mother told me not to bother him too much.

On the morning of January third, we started hearing rumors that Noriega was caving in, that it would only be a matter of days now before he walked out and the Americans took him into their custody. Thousands of Panamanians were demonstrating in front of the Vatican Embassy, demanding that he surrender. It was starting to seem like he might. Reina had gone back to work and called from her office to give us updates.

"Is it the music?" I asked her on the phone. The Americans had been blaring their rock music in the general direction of the embassy for days now, thinking that maybe it would be annoying enough that Noriega would have to come out. I still hadn't been downtown, but Reina said that you could feel the bass vibrations through the pavement. Everyone in the city was making jokes about it.

"The music was an idiot's idea," she said. "He's probably dancing in there."

In light of what Reina reported, my mother suggested we make something nice for dinner together. I didn't really want to. Just hearing that it might be over soon made me feel like it already was, and I had the urge to go out somewhere, to see people and be back in the city.

"Okay, you can go somewhere," my mother said. "Now where should that be?" She tapped her front teeth with her fingernail. I could tell she had something in mind. "I know. You can go to the supermarket. They must be open by now. I'll give you a list." She turned to grab a pencil and a napkin to write on. "And, Ramón," she said, "these are not things that can be plucked off a tree in a neighbor's yard."

She had known all along about the limes. But instead of feeling found out, I was happy to be reminded of something from a time when everything had been better for us. It seemed like we were headed back to that.

I returned from the Supermarket Rey with beef roast, tomato paste, limes, lettuce, tomatoes, a small burlap sack of rice, and Baturro salsa—the ingredients for *lomo*, my father's favorite meal. I also bought Tabasco, even though my mother forgot to include it on the list, because I knew my father had been missing it. It felt good to have food in the house again and my mother and I started a countdown to time ourselves against when everyone would come home.

"How was it out there?" she asked.

"It seemed okay. I mean, there was trash everywhere and some of the windows were broken at the shops. And the whole supermarket smelled like fish. But it was okay."

"The fish has probably been rotting in there for days. The smell will go away eventually, though." She wiped down the counter with circular strokes, readying a surface for us to work on.

We started making the food in the late afternoon. By the time both Tito and Reina arrived home, my mother was scraping the burnt rice—her favorite part—from the bottom of the *paila* and it seemed we had timed everything perfectly. I was instructed to set the table and Reina cooed over the prospect of having our first real meal in weeks. We all sat down to wait for my father. After a while, Tito asked me to fill his glass and my mother said I might as well fill all of them. The glasses had been overturned to keep out flies but I gathered them now and poured everyone some water. I put a plastic coaster over my father's.

Reina was squirming in her seat, anxious to eat, and finally Tito said that they should go ahead. "Probably more mayhem at the hospital," he said. "Who knows when he'll be home."

The meat was tender and juicy as I pulled it apart with my fork and swirled it into my rice. I swear my stomach almost hurt eating it. I could only finish a little.

Reina was telling Tito again what she had already told us that morning.

He shook his head. "It's going to be the beginning of a lot of things soon," he said, pointing his fork at Reina. "I can almost guarantee you we're going to be making more money from now on. For a long time, *mami*. There's so much construction to be done now. Here in San Miguelito, whole roads need to be rebuilt. I'm going to have a lot of jobs coming at me."

Suddenly, my mother pushed herself from the table. The metal legs of her chair squeaked against the floor. "Oh my God," she said.

"You left something in the oven?" Reina asked, grinning.

"Francisco," my mother murmured. She was staring

across the room with wide eyes as if she were watching a ghost dancing on the wall. Her hands gripped the lip of the table. I looked to where she stared, but saw nothing.

"What's wrong?" Tito asked.

My mother stood and ran to her bedroom.

"Ramón, what's wrong with her?" Tito asked.

"I don't know," I said.

She came back a few seconds later with a piece of white cloth clasped in her hand.

"Where are your keys?" she demanded of Tito.

He patted his pants pocket. "Right here."

My mother was hardly blinking. "We have to go," she said.

"Now, Mariella—" Reina started.

"We have to go," she said again.

Tito stood and put his hands on her shoulders but she shuddered away.

"Please," she said, and even from where I was sitting, I could see an animal desperation in her eyes, gleaming and bright.

"Okay," he said. My mother claimed she could drive herself but Tito reminded her she hadn't driven in almost five years and it was *his* car so he would drive.

Reina insisted on going, too. "I want to see what's gotten into her now," she said.

Tito said, "Everyone goes," and my mother had the most excruciated look on her face, as if that was the last thing she wanted but all she said was, "Hurry, we have to hurry."

In the car, Tito asked where we were going, but my mother wouldn't say. She simply gave directions from the front seat, shaking and telling Tito to speed up at nearly every turn. It became clear, after a while, that we were headed to our old house. And then I remembered what I couldn't believe I hadn't earlier: Today was the day it was scheduled to be torn down. I knew then what my mother had realized only an hour before: My father was there, watching it happen.

We were stopped by American guards at two road-blocks along the way and then waved through. As we neared our old street, I had the sudden fear that maybe our house had already been destroyed during the inva-sion. I half-expected to see an empty lot, razed to noth-ing but rubble. But as we turned the corner, there it was—the terra-cotta-colored shutters straight along-side the windows, the wavy clay-tiled roof, the small front patio with turquoise twisting columns reaching from an outer ledge to the ceiling, the cracked cement driveway with tufts of grass poking through. One bull-dozer faced it from the street, ready to go to work, and one crane with a wrecking ball hummed in the yard. The land was scattered with hundreds of fluorescent marker flags and spray-paint ticks, but otherwise, it looked the same. It was good to see it again.

Before Tito had even turned off the car, my mother jumped out. "Where is he?" she asked to the air. She started walking toward the back of the house, calling my father's name.

"Your mother's gone crazy, Ramón," Reina said.

My mother was swallowed behind the house, probably still yelling, when a foreman came over and told us we needed to distance ourselves from the property.

"It's not safe here," he warned. They would be starting the demolition in about ten minutes and only the crew was allowed on the premises.

Tito said a few things to the foreman about how of course we understood and he himself was in construction and was quite familiar with the rules of operation and he assured the foreman we would get my mother back in the car shortly and then leave.

A few minutes later, when a loud horn bleated into the twilight air, Tito said he was going to get her. "This is stupid," he said. "Francisco's probably at home, eating all our *lomo*."

Reina sighed and sat down in the car, leaving the door open and her legs dangling out. "It's incredible that you turned out so well, Ramón, with a mother like that. She's always been crazy, you know."

I looked at Reina in the shadows of the car. Her hair was piled atop her head like cotton candy, dried out and sprayed stiff. Her face would have been more attractive without the green eye shadow she layered on each morning and the scarlet lipstick. She and Tito had lived with my parents since before I was born but I had never been that close to them. Physical nearness does not necessarily breed intimacy. I thought about what Tito had said at dinner, about making lots of money soon, and I wondered if they would get their own house at last. Reina accused everyone else of being weak but she was the one still clinging on, still using her brother as a crutch. There was weakness there, though she would be the last to admit it.

Finally, I said, "Crazy is better than cruel." I felt the tension that comes from willful disregard course through me, as if I were tightening myself against a blow that I knew was coming.

Reina looked at me evenly. I thought she was coming up with what to say in return, something that would level me, but she only blinked quickly a few times and turned away.

Tito came back around, shouting, "Is Mariella out here? Did she come back this way?"

Reina and I both shook our heads.

"I can't find her," Tito said.

"She has to be in there somewhere," Reina said. "This is ridiculous."

"I'm going to find the foreman. They can't start until we find her." Tito walked off.

Reina leaned her head back, closing her eyes. I wandered to the side of the house and was headed to the rear, to where our clothesline used to hang above the roosters that strutted through the dirt, when, like a flash through the window, I saw them. My father was seated on the floor in my parents' old bedroom. It used to be his parents' room and his grandparents' before that. He was dressed in his work clothes—white pants and a royal blue polo shirt with the name of the hospital embroidered on the breast. His ID badge hung around his neck. He had taken off his shoes. My mother knelt beside him, holding his hand. I couldn't quite make out what they were saying, but it looked like they were praying. After another minute, a horn again bleated into the darkness. My mother was crying now. My father took her and kissed her and brushed her hair back with his hand. Then she stood up and ran out. I stayed long enough to watch my father lay down on the floor and then ran out into the front yard, too. When she saw me, she said, "What did you see?"

I stared at her blankly.

"You know, don't you?" she said.

I thought maybe I did but I said, "What?" because I wanted to believe that I was wrong, I wanted her to say something that would prove me wrong.

Instead, she started crying again. She wiped her cheeks with the white cloth she had been clenching in her hand since we left Cerro Viento. It was the handkerchief my father had given her the first time they met.

"Where have you been?" Tito walked up to us. "They need to start." He pulled us down the driveway and out to the street.

"Mariella," he said. "Don't be so upset. You have a perfectly good new house now. This is only one part of your life, right?"

It was something that used to be true but wouldn't be soon. The house was only one part of her life once, a house she moved into after she got married, a house she loved in its own way, but a house she brought herself to leave. When my father died in there, though, it would no longer simply be part of her life, or mine. Most of our lives—the best part—would be gone with it. For my father, though, it had always been different. That house was everything. He had the history of lifetimes behind him there. He had never spent a night sleeping anywhere else. Every single thing that ever truly mattered to him in some way had to do with being there. There wasn't a world for him outside of it. And so— though this was a level of acceptance I was able to come to only years later—it made sense that he would want to die in that house. Little by little, he was already dying outside of it. He hadn't let on. At first, he had seemed depressed but still he had been able to go to work, to eat with us, to love us. But every day, every second since leaving, something vital inside him must have been wilting away, small and drooping, folding into itself and withering. I thought, and sometimes still think, that it was unforgivably selfish to leave us like that. But sometimes I wonder if it wouldn't have been equally selfish to ask him to exist in a world that for him held no color, no sound, no taste, no *life*, for no other reason than to be with us.

My mother was stony-faced when she turned to look at the house. The rumble of the bulldozer started and Tito put an arm around my mother's shoulder. "It's probably better that Francisco's not here to see this," he said.

I looked to my mother, but her face gave away nothing. I couldn't believe she was going to let this happen. We stood and watched as the wrecking ball swung out slowly, almost gracefully, and then hurtled into the house, where the office used to be. Pieces of the roof caved in and cracked like thunder. Puffs of dirt rose up and dispersed in the twilight sky. I was breathing fast, the air getting caught in my throat, and I felt a tremendous electric twitch all through my body. I had the thought, I don't know why, that I could run to the laundromat and buy a gun from the guys who had set up their table in the alley. I could run back and hold it up to the construction workers' heads and tell them to stop. I could tell them my father was in there.

The ball swung again, like a bird swooping through

the sky, and then crashed through another corner and fell back.

"I can't believe it. Finally," Reina said from behind us. My mother stood absolutely still.

I looked over my shoulder to Reina and almost said it. I could feel the words collecting in my mouth. I heard the wrecking ball machine repositioning behind me and turned to watch it creep backward, shift to the right a little, and then stop again, ready for the next hit.

"Mamá!" I yelled above the growl of the machines. I was pleading with her to stop this, because I thought she was the only one who could. But she swallowed hard and grabbed my hand, squeezing my fingers together until I could feel the bones touching.

"Do you want to leave?" Tito shouted at me.

My mother kneaded her fingertips into my palm as if warning me to stay quiet, telling me to trust her. But my chest felt constricted and tired and as if it was breaking like brittle straw. Tears were worming in my eyes. And, finally, I couldn't help it.

"He's in there!" I screamed. As soon as I said it, something shattered in me. I started sobbing. It rushed up from my belly and from my toes, from all the quiet pools in me, and gushed out.

"What?" Tito asked, leaning toward me and squinting. My mother said, "Nothing."

"He's inside!" I said again.

Tito dropped his arm from Mariella's shoulder and turned to her. "What do you mean, he's inside?"

My mother was silent. I fell onto the pavement, pebbles pressing against my legs, and wept. I felt so weak, like my legs had turned to string, totally collapsible. I heard Tito call my father's name and when I looked up, he was sprinting across the street, waving his arms. He was frantically shouting but as he got closer to the house, I could no longer hear him, and I knew the workers wouldn't either.

Reina stood and was wailing. She grabbed my mother's arms and dug her nails into them, leaving little half-moons up and down my mother's flesh. "How could you do this?" she screamed. "What are you doing?" Bits of spit flew into my mother's face and she shook my mother's thin body, as if she were trying to loosen something from a box, as if there were answers inside my mother that would come out if she shook hard enough. But my mother just looked ahead, her eyes like marbles, watching the bulldozer push in now, watching, as I did through tear-soaked eyes, chunks of the cement walls tumble in and fall unto themselves in piles amid a haze of dust that wafted in the air like fog.

JANUARY 4, 1990
Noriega surrendered that day but we didn't know it until the middle of the night, when a symphony of

honking horns erupted in the streets and we learned, from a neighbor, that he was probably being loaded onto an American plane at that very moment, and that he would be taken to the United States for a trial. It hardly seemed to matter. We were outside the exhilaration that everyone else reveled in, lost in the morass of our own private mourning.

Flor called in the middle of the night, eager to share her jubilation at Noriega's surrender. Tito answered the phone. He told her my father was dead. She wanted to talk to my mother, but my mother wasn't talking. When she got home, she had fallen in a heap on the floor beside her bed. She had walked all the way to Cerro Viento, by herself, and hadn't spoken to anyone since. Reina had pleaded with her to stop it, had cursed her for letting it happen. My mother screamed out once—a high and piercing scream that vibrated to the pit of my stomach—saying, "He wants to stay in the house! He wants this!" She shrieked it as if she was trying to make sure the sound got all the way to heaven, all the way to God, so that He would know. Then she fell silent again.

Ubi called in the morning. Everything in the newspaper was about Noriega, but buried in the back was a small obituary for my father. Reina had been able to get it in right away, through a friend at her office.

"Where was he?" Ubi asked.

"In La Chorrera," I lied. I didn't want to tell him the truth: that my father had willed himself to die.

"I'm sorry," he said. "My mother and I will come to the funeral."

I didn't know whether there would be a funeral, but I told him thanks. "Your mother's okay? I talked to her the other day."

"I know, she told me. She's going to be fine." He was quiet.

"And Sofia?" I asked.

"Ramón, I'm so—"

"I sent her a postcard telling her how I felt. It was before I knew." I almost started crying again right then. "You have to get it for me. It will go to her family's box but you have to get it. Please."

"Sure."

"Throw it away."

He was quiet.

"Ubi?"

"Okay."

As it turned out, there wasn't a proper funeral. Reina wanted to go back to the house and find what was left of his body and bury it. My mother was still on the floor, balled up like a blanket that had fallen off the bed in the middle of the night, unable or else unwilling to speak. I spoke for her.

"He wanted to stay in the house," I told Reina, standing up to her like a man, acting like I had seen my father act so many times—solemn and assured.

She looked shocked. "Don't you want to bury him?"

Tito came up behind her and put a hand on her shoulder. He looked awful—we all did—his face puffy and pale, his wavy dark hair uncombed and out of place.

"No," I said. Reina's face sunk. "He's already been cremated. Most of the time, when people are cremated, you throw their ashes out into the sea or onto some piece of land that they had a connection with. His ashes are already in their place." I had been thinking about this a lot. It made me feel better for some reason to think of it that way.

Reina shook her head. "That's bullshit," she said. "He should have been buried."

JANUARY 8, 1990

We had a memorial service for my father at our old church later that week. We tacked photographs of him onto a piece of foam and put it on an easel in the front of the church. People I had never seen in my life streamed in and out for hours, stopping to kiss my cheeks and say they were sorry. I wondered how many of these people knew how he had died, as if that mattered. The priest spoke once, but I was hardly listening. Reina, Flor, and Tito stood at a different door than my mother and I, only the beginning of the ways they would distance themselves from my mother in the years to come and shut her out. To them, what my mother had allowed was indefensible. I was furious at her, too, and confused, furious at every single thing about it. But even then I think I was able to recognize something of love in what she had done.

Ubi came with his mother. We hugged, something I don't think we had ever done. Sofia came later, by herself. I felt a tremendous apprehension at seeing her again.

"Ubaldo told me," she said. "I'm so sorry, Ramón."

She kissed both my cheeks. I breathed in the smell of her skin and didn't let it out until my chest burned. I told her thank you and watched her walk out, her skirt hitting at her knobby knees, her sandals clapping as she moved. I felt the most indescribable loss then. The weight of everything—the past weeks, my father, Sofia—dropped through my body like a crashing elevator. I felt hollowed and dulled, hazy around the edges and empty inside. For the rest of the day, I shook everyone's hands and nodded my head absently.

And then, at one point, I looked up and everything was radiant. In Panama, at funerals, everyone wears white. I had learned that at my grandfather's funeral when I was a little boy. Everyone who filed in that day had on white pants, white shirts, white skirts and dresses, white shoes, white silk scarves, white hats, white ties, white polyester, white nylon, white cotton. The church was filled with people reverently moving through the pews, a sea of white. Sunlight streamed through the tall, thin windows and fell over everyone like a halo. In the midst of it all I had the thought that it was like being in heaven, among angels. And that surely my father was there. I knew he was one of them.

APRIL 24, 2000

Our lives fell apart after that, crumbling in on us like the house, like buildings all over Panama in the aftermath of the invasion. Tito and Reina moved out as soon as they were able to find an apartment. I never heard another word that either of them uttered, except that night after the memorial, when I lay in my bed, and Reina walked in and knelt beside me and, in a fierce whisper, said, "This was your fault, too, Ramón. You knew!" and I could feel her hot breath against my face. I kept my eyes closed, pretending to be asleep. "You killed your father, Ramón," she said. She stayed there, staring at me for a few minutes in the dark.

When they moved to their new apartment, my mother lost our house in Cerro Viento. There was no way to make the payments on her own. At least that's what she told me. But one night, before we left, as we sat at the table eating cheese on bread and fried yucca, she produced a slip of green paper from under the phone book in a kitchen drawer.

"I have something for you," she said. Her skin had grown wrinkled. She washed her face at night with milk of magnesia, but she never wore makeup anymore, even though she had never worn a lot. Her hair was limp and oily. Her eyes were tired and interminably sad. She carried my father's handkerchief with her everywhere, sometimes using it to dab her tearing eyes or sometimes just holding it to her nose, as though the scent of my father was mingled in the fibers.

She passed the green paper across the table. It was a check. A check from the Zoña Construction Company for twenty thousand dollars.

"I didn't tell your father. He would have torn it up, you know. But I want you to have it. I want you to go to the United States and go to college."

"I can go to college here."

She shook her head. "This isn't a life for you."

"Yes it is. This is my life. There isn't another one. Mamá, you could use the money here. We could use it. You could keep this house."

"No," she said. "It wouldn't be right. To build a new life here without your father. With *that* money. In *this* house."

Then I understood. "You want to lose it," I said.

"I can't stay here." She pulled her hands back over her hair, matting it down.

"We could both go to the United States," I said, though I knew she would refuse.

She looked straight at me. The yellow light hummed above us. "I saved your life once," she said. "I know nobody thinks of it that way."

"I do," I said.

She smiled. "I just want to do it again."

I was too young for college yet, but my mother found a boarding school in Pennsylvania that would take me, and then I would go to college when I had my high school diploma. What seemed like a lot of money in Panama didn't go very far in the United States and by the time I enrolled at Lehigh University, I had to find a part-time job to support myself. I worked as a box crusher and a stock boy at the local supermarket for four years, coming home with tiny cuts on my hands where the razor blade had slipped, my back aching from standing up for hours at a time. There were days when I thought my life here wasn't much different than it would have been if I had stayed in Panama. But then I met my future wife in college, a nursing student from

New Jersey who almost made me stop breathing the moment I saw her. Her name was Margaret, and when I told my mother about her, she was pleased because Margaret was the name of a saint.

Ubi married Sofia. I heard that from my mother, even though every once in a while, Ubi or I would telephone each other. I sent them a card, wishing them every happiness, and a gift—a set of encyclopedias for the children I knew they would have. I put a note in the inside cover of the first volume: "So your kids don't have to fish their knowledge from trash cans, like someone I used to know."

My mother spent the years moving from apartment to apartment. Twice, during the construction of the new high-rise on our old lot, she went and slept on the newly laid cement, amid the giant machines at rest for the night.

"I thought it would make me feel closer to him," she explained. "But it didn't. I feel him all the time, anyway."

I called her every Sunday and wired her money once a month, though I didn't know what she did with it. She talked in the past, never about where she had gone that day or whom she had seen or what she would do tomorrow, but always about the two weeks during the invasion, always about my father.

The last time I spoke to her, she told me she had heard him. "I was buying bananas," she said, "and I heard his voice behind me, singing. You know his song.

To dream the impossible dream. Ramón," she told me, "I know I didn't hear it. I'm not going crazy. But I can't tell you how badly I wanted to hear it."

It was only three days later when Ubi called me to tell me she had died. His mother was the one who told him. It was in her sleep. It was peaceful.

I hadn't been back to Panama in ten years. I thought I was carrying it all with me but as soon as Margaret and I landed at the airport, I felt a shock run through me. The swampy air, the unrelenting sun, the smell of exhaust clinging to everything. The pockmarked faces of the men at the car rental counter. The constant surge of traffic. The glint of the lights from city buildings against the water in the evening. The rumbling buses airbrushed with images of celebrities or landscapes. *Panaderías, lavanderías, carnecerías* on almost every corner. The Supermarket Rey, the Casa de la Carne, a new place called Mattito's. Cars honking, jackhammers hammering. Broken pavement. Swarms of schoolchildren, all in uniform, huddled in front of Wendy's and Kentucky Fried Chicken. People hobbling through stopped traffic, selling dish towels, newspapers, roses. Men returning crates of glass bottles for a refund. Neon lights turned on even during the day. The graceful lean and sway of palm trees hovering over it all. My blood rushed in a kind of nervous excitement at being in the place to which my soul was connected, at being home.

The funeral was in the same church my father's had been. When we walked in almost no one was there. It reminded me of walking into Christmas Eve Mass that year. My mother had left a will in which she asked to be cremated and for her ashes to be scattered by her husband's. Later, I would return for the first time to where our house used to be and, with only Margaret looking on, I would pour the ashes into the first sign of dirt at the edge of the concrete parking garage attached to the high-rise there, turning over the soil with my hands.

Ubi and Sofia came to the church, along with Ubi's mother. Ubi had a mustache now and I teased him, saying it was about time. Sofia was still thin, and taller now, but what had once been an unusual loveliness had transformed into unqualified radiance. Even so, I could tell she was the kind of woman who didn't comprehend her own beauty. I introduced them all to Margaret. Her hair had curled from the humidity and in a fit of frustration that morning at the hotel she had pulled it back. She didn't like how she looked, I knew, but even next to Sofia, she was the most gorgeous woman I had ever seen. After a few more minutes, our former priest, who had retired, arrived to say Mass as a favor to my mother. We waited for half an hour after the funeral was supposed to begin but neither Flor nor Tito nor Reina ever showed up.

The priest was going to say a few words and then I was supposed to get up to deliver the eulogy. Margaret held my hand as I waited. Life had killed my father, and then my mother, in heartbreak, had died because of him. Or maybe it was like Reina once said: Maybe my mother and I killed my father, but in return he killed a little bit of both of us. I kept thinking about it, but I suppose it didn't matter what exactly had happened and who was to blame. "God will take care," my father always said. Whether in this life or the next. And I believed him.

The priest called my name. Margaret squeezed my hand. For days, I hadn't been sure what I would say. But I would talk about heaven, I thought then, and how I saw it in this church once, so I know it exists. I would talk about God's arms growing infinitely longer so as to be able to hold all of us in His embrace. And I would tell my story—about my mother and my father and me—and how in that story was all that I knew about love.

Acknowledgments

With enormous thanks to Kate Lee, agent extraordinaire, for being the best ally any writer could hope for; my brilliant editor, Megan Lynch, for believing in me from the start; Chris Offutt, for making me believe in myself; Frank Conroy, Marilynne Robinson, Lan Samantha Chang, and Elizabeth McCracken; Ted Genoways, for giving me my first big break and being a generous advocate ever since; Susan Hahn and Ian Morris; Susan Burmeister-Brown and Linda Swanson-Davies; Deborah Treisman, Cressida Leyshon, and Mike Peed; Celina Barkema Vargas, for sharing her story; Kate Sullivan and Diana Spechler, for being incredible readers and even better friends; Stefan Grudza, for getting me started; Erin Hogan, for guiding me; my parents, for patiently answering all my millions of questions and for their love; and Ryan Kowalczyk, for everything always.

About the Author

CRISTINA HENRÍQUEZ is a graduate of the Iowa Writers' Workshop and a recipient of the Alfredo Cisneros del Moral Foundation Award, and was featured in *The Virginia Quarterly Review* as one of Fiction's New Luminaries. Her stories have been published in *The New Yorker, Glimmer Train, TriQuarterly,* and *AGNI.* She lives with her husband in Chicago.